AMNESTY

THE REVOLT TRILOGY
BY BENJAMIN VOGT

REVOLT
Book One

MUTINY
Book Two

AMNESTY

BENJAMIN VOGT

Copyright © 2022 by Benjamin Vogt

Cover © 2022 by Benjamin Vogt

Published by Kyburg Publishing

Editing and Formatting by Stacey Smekofske at EditByStacey.com

Cover Design by Shandy Vogt

ISBN: 978-1-7337650-5-3 Paperback

978-1-7337650-8-4 eBook

All rights reserved.

No part of this book may be reproduced in any form or by any electronic or mechanical means, including information storage and retrieval systems, without written permission from the author, except for the use of brief quotations in a book review.

To Natalie. You're the Chloe to my Jason, and I love you with all my heart.

CHAPTER ONE

The fortress with thick, cold concrete walls stands erect against the dark sky. A tall chain-link fence surrounds its perimeter, and at the front entrance, two Reapers hold leashes to keep their dogs in check.

A little over a month ago, Mills ordered that Fenway Park be converted into a base of operations. The once accommodating structure now resembles a bastion. A tank could fire a missile at its foundation and the inhabitants inside wouldn't lose a wink of sleep.

How our bastard President survived getting his throat slit is beyond me. His flesh tore. My blade rippled through his jugular. He had to have used Rebirth—the serum that brings the dead back to life; the serum that knits you back together piece by piece.

The same serum I've used time and time again.

Exodus stands by my side atop a major business complex opposite the super fortress. He's dressed like a Saint: jet-black combat boots, gray camo pants, and a black tactical vest over a skintight combat shirt. His messy white hair is concealed by a ski mask pulled down over his pale face.

I search for Raphael, finding him prone on the snow-covered

rooftop with a sniper rifle tucked up against his shoulder. His sights are on the two Reapers guarding the front of the complex. His right eye peers through the scope—his left is probably closed, but with the charred, black metallic material morphed into that area of his face, it's only an assumption.

It's been a bit since the events of Seattle. . . since the night Chloe was taken. After Kennedy was murdered by my doppelgänger, and we discovered the sinister reality of what had happened, we ran faster than we ever had before. We made it to the rendezvous point where the remaining members of Lazarus were waiting for us, then we left. They had tried sending a message out to the rest of America, but security was too tight, and with all the panic from the mist closing in, Dante called it quits and ordered everyone to the trucks—allowing Mills to pin the whole damn thing on us. After escaping, we went to Nevada. There, Dante held a meeting, voicing his concerns over our diminished numbers. We couldn't make a change without an appropriate source of followers and supplies. He took what remained of Lazarus and set off to recruit more souls willing to fight. Raphael, Exodus, and I were left to find Chloe.

We haven't heard from Dante in over a month.

"Jay," Raphael mutters. His focus is still on the two Elites.

"You have your mask on? We only have a small window to do this."

"Yeah, I'm all ready to go," I affirm.

"Good, start rappelling."

A black rope is anchored to an exhaust vent a couple feet away. Exodus and I grab the end of each of our ropes and loop them through the carabiners attached to our harnesses, securing them for descent.

Exodus sighs, "Breaking out of Salem made me hate crap like this."

"You were the one who said climbing down was our only option."

"Still," he mumbles

"You'll be fine. Just stick to the plan." I tightly grip the rope with my gloved hands.

We step over to the ledge. My brain swishes to the blanket of snow beneath us. It's at least 200 feet away, but that doesn't matter.

Nothing's going to stop me from getting to her, not after everything we've been through.

I cast my gaze about, scanning for threats.

Boston. The place where it all started.

"Jason, I'm being serious," Raphael mutters.

"Don't get your panties in a twist." Leaning out over the void, my body is now just beyond a 45-degree angle.

With one last breath, I push away from the building. The rope slows my descent.

After Dante left, we desperately clawed at any trace of Chloe. Through hacking CCTV cameras, we were able to track down a man named Isaac Wells, a *popular* bureaucrat in Mills' Government.

We stalked him for days, learning all there was to know. We found out where he worked, how he got there, and what time he left. We even found out which room his ten-year-old son slept in, what nights he and his much younger wife went out, and which windows were left unlocked.

Once our confidence in his routine grew, we struck, killing his armed security and abducting him on his way home from work.

We did unspeakable things to him, and you know what? I regret absolutely nothing. I wouldn't sleep until I knew Chloe was alive, and he was the answer to all my prayers. After starving him, mutilating his body, and threatening his family, he broke. Putting his three-fingered hand out, he begged us to stop. He told us she was here, at Fenway Park. She was being held in some underground torture chamber. The sickos even had live footage streaming to the phones of Mills' upper subordinates. I took

Issacs's cell, and after receiving detailed instructions on how to enter the stream, I saw exactly where she was and what they were doing to her.

The anger was enough to immediately put a bullet in his head.

Flames replace the blood soaring through my veins. My feet crunch against the snow, now at ground level.

I'll make all of them pay.

Exodus lands by my side.

We detach the rope and toss our harnesses.

"What if they notice?" Exodus asks, pointing to the back of my leg.

Glancing back at the blood stain, I recall the bullet I lodged into the Saint's hamstring before violently strangling him to death and stealing his uniform, "They won't, and if they do, Raphael will take care of it."

"Jay, we don't want Raphael to do *anything* if he doesn't have to."

"I don't think they'll have time to notice the blood with what's about to happen. Okay, Blaine?"

"If you say so."

We adjust our clothing and head to the main entrance. The wind picks up, and more snow gradually falls from the sky.

The fortress looms in the February night; the top of the structure hidden by falling snow. We stop in our tracks as the leashed dogs growl.

The man in front of me mirrors my height. His trench coat sways in the wind, and his black gas mask hides his facial expression. His large frame is protected by a tactical shotgun gripped in his hands; the leash restraining his dog is wrapped around his left wrist.

"Who are you two?" he asks. His modulated voice sounds like nails on a chalkboard. "I don't recall any additions to tonight's roster."

Exodus answers, "We weren't supposed to be here. We were

on checkpoint duty, but we got a call over coms for something important."

"Which is?"

"We don't know."

The two Reapers exchange looks as their dogs get louder.

The cold, dark night Simon and I went to Nacht-fest appears fresh in my mind. One of the military dogs latched onto his arm and tore into it like a steak. A rock was used to smash its face in.

The other Reaper points to a small device next to him that's mounted to a tripod, "Scan your prints, then show us your ID."

Exodus goes first, taking off his right glove. He glances down at his finger before placing it on the device.

A chime rings out.

My confidence is bolstered by his success. Pulling off my left glove, I glance down at my finger. The gel smeared across it is still there. I scan my print, and an identical chime rings out.

We don our gloves once more. Next step is showing our ID's, but before we get to that, the device flashes red and has a complete meltdown, shrilling.

The Reapers frantically push buttons on the machine. Their dogs' howls match the new high pitched shriek.

"System error?" one asks. He cocks his head to the side.

The screen goes black. The other pulls out his radio, "We have a system error out front on our scanner. I need someone to run a diagnostic check, asap."

A moment goes by with no response, the wind howling in our ears. Eventually, a crackled reply comes over the com, "Yeah, we're having some problems on our end too. Security cams and the network are both down. Stand by."

Exodus groans, "We don't have time for this."

The other Reaper hisses, "Keep your mouth shut."

"But it's cold."

"Cold? You're cold? How about—"

The same voice pours through the radio again, "Yeah, no,

everything is completely offline—must be the storm. Was there anyone trying to use the scanner when it went down?"

The first Reaper replies, "Yes, two Saints saying that they were called in for something important."

"What are their names? I think I know who you're talking about."

Without being asked, Exodus and I pull out our ID's and present them to the two Elites. The Reapers examine them.

One raises the radio back to his mouth, "Liam Irons, and Ryland Yarborough."

Silence.

"I can't be a positive, but I believe those two are here for a meeting with Robyn," the voice on the radio flatly states.

The Reapers laugh, the metallic screech harmonizing with the wind, "May God have mercy on their souls."

My left eye twitches.

Those have been the last words to so many people I've cared about, including myself.

"You can say that again," the voice mutters. "Let them pass and tell them that her office is on the third floor; rear left."

"Copy that."

He tucks his radio away, shaking his head and stepping to the side. "All right, you heard him, third floor, rear left office."

Their dogs snarl as we stride past them. My hands ball up into fists at my side. Once we reach the two heavy metal doors that serve as the entrance to the fortress, I grab a handle and heave it open.

A long and wide corridor goes on for about a hundred yards before a staircase leads both up and down.

It doesn't resemble the old stadium in the slightest. Sports weren't allowed, but Fenway was left standing because it served as a good amphitheater for Mills when he wanted to hold speeches or make major announcements.

I don't think there's been a baseball game in the US for over thirty years. My only knowledge of it stems from memories my dad recollected from his youth.

"Do you think she's still in the lower levels?" Exodus asks as we make our way down the corridor.

"She'd better be."

"But if she's not?"

I ignore him. Without hesitation, we start down the stairs that lead to the bowels of the fortress.

Where are all the guards? Why isn't there any security? Something isn't right.

Forty steps down, we enter a different section. Doors litter each side of the long and wide walkway. Another flight of stairs waits in the back.

"I know you probably want me to shut up," Exodus says, keeping pace with me. "But I'm feeling nervous. Who's this Robyn-dude? Why did the Reapers act like we were walking to our deaths when they heard that?"

He has a valid point. I know that I should logically feel the same way, but all I can focus on is Chloe. She's been gone for so long.

I've been torn from her. She's been torn from me. We are one and the same. I'm broken when she's not by my side.

We're about to reach the stairs when a scream pierces the silence. Our heads turn in unison. It came from beyond a door ahead. A small window is in the center of it.

I peer inside.

"What the hell?" I mutter.

There's a naked woman strapped to a gurney, wildly thrashing against her restraints as two men in lab coats inject elongated needles into her flesh, pumping her full of some unknown liquid. She screams harder, and even though I'm shocked at the sight, my heart relaxes when I see it isn't Chloe.

But it could be if I don't hurry.

I turn back toward the stairs, leaving Exodus at the window. Suddenly, he lets out an audible gasp.

My gaze shoots back to the woman. Black liquid streams from her eyes, and one of the men tightens the restraints against her writhing body. My stomach churns as the other takes a wicked looking baton and viscously beats her, raining blows upon her head.

I cringe, grabbing Exodus by the arm, tearing him away from the horror in that room.

"Focus," I say, stepping down the first step. "Look, there's the door."

"Bingo. Just like the one from the live stream." Exodus sounds a little shaken.

I'm calm on the exterior, but on the inside my adrenaline, anticipation, anger, fear, and much more complex emotions have me on edge. The girl I love is on the other side of that door, and in just a moment I'll be able to set her free.

I picture her emerald, green eyes, and her beautiful blond hair.

"Get ready." I pull my handgun out of its holster and flip the safety off.

Exodus does the same. The two of us reach the bottom step.

My heart hammers. I wonder if it's loud enough to give us away.

"One."

I reach for the knob on the door.

"Two."

I grasp and twist.

"Three."

I throw the door open, swinging my gun and wrapping my finger around the trigger.

Nobody. . . not a single soul.

No.

No, no, no, no, no.

My breathing hastens. I storm into the room, scanning

everything. A corner lamp provides meager lighting to the room, and scribbled writing on a white board is barely visible. Blood coats a wooden chair and concrete floor in the center of it all.

It's still wet.

I see nothing but red; flames ignite inside my chest.

"Calm down," Exodus urges. I grab the chair and hurl it against the wall. It bursts into pieces.

I grit my teeth. "Calm down? Our only chance to get her is *gone!*"

He points to a large camera attached to a tripod near the front of the room, "Someone was in here not too long ago. Check the footage."

Unchecked murderous rage festers inside of me. I examine the large camera. A yellow sticky note is attached to its screen.

"Come read this," I mutter. My dyslexia is worse when I'm upset. "I can't right now."

Exodus stares at the note, then reads, "Footage uploaded. Robyn has Frye."

Robyn. Who is this guy?

The white board catches my attention. "Let's check that out."

He nods.

At the top right of the board, a picture of Mills is covered in black lip prints.

"What does it say?" I ask.

Exodus exhales, "Damn. . ."

"What?"

"My Lord and Savior. I love you. Let me carry your seed. The Maiden's Touch will be the end before the beginning. Jason Pinder must die."

Befuddlement drowns my anger, "The Maiden's Touch?"

"I have no idea."

My focus narrows. Blood rushes through my ears as I clench my jaw. "She's gotta still be here somewhere. Maybe she's up on the third level in Robyn's office?"

"Jason. . ." Exodus trails off. "I know you don't want to hear this, but our window is closing. Those cameras will be back on any minute now. We don't know that Chloe is up there, and if we get caught, we're no good to her anyway. We've got to get out of here, get back to the motel, and figure some crap out, all right? It's not what you want but it's what has to happen, dude."

I swallow the hopes of rescuing her tonight. I've been punched in the gut.

"You're right. We need to get back to Raph and tell him about this. This and what they were doing to that woman upstairs."

"Something's definitely going on."

"Agreed.

CHAPTER TWO

Making our way back through the facility is off-putting. There's still no sign of any Saints patrolling, and the woman strapped to the gurney along with her two torturers are no longer behind that door.

"It's way too quiet," Exodus says. I share his apprehension.

But still. . . I can't get Chloe out of my head. I failed. I was supposed to save her tonight. I was supposed to be holding her right now, telling her that I'd never leave her behind.

I'm not alive when she isn't here.

I'm lost. Just an empty, twisted shell of a man.

She truly completed me. I'd do anything for her—kill anyone.

I grit my teeth and stop in my tracks.

Exodus turns, "What are you doing? We need to leave."

I debate turning around and shooting my way through this hellhole, "She was supposed to be here."

"She isn't dead, though. That's what matters most."

"But why? Why haven't they killed her, yet?"

"I—" he stumbles for a moment, shaking his head. "I don't know. I really don't, but I feel like we're being watched, so can we please—"

"Yeah," I swallow. I need to collect myself or I'm dead. "We can get out of here."

With more haste in our step, we advance through the stadium.

"I'm not trying to be insensitive, man," he continues. "It's just—I was in Salem for years and years, and if there was one thing that place taught me, it's that some people have a sixth sense that warns them when crap is about to go down. And right now, that little alarm is going off inside my head."

I nod, and we head up the second flight of stair to the main floor.

"I know. I'm hearing the same thing." I finally answer.

We reach the top. The facility is like a mausoleum, utterly silent and devoid of life. No Saints, no nothing. We hurry our way down the corridor toward the main entrance, looming ahead.

A loud chirp rings out from a sound system above. The two of us freeze.

Another chirp. My breathing accelerates. We wait for an eternity of uncomfortable silence. Eventually, my lips allow themselves to move.

"What was that?"

"I don't know. It could be a lot of things."

"Maybe it was the security system booting back up?"

He takes a few steps forward, stops for a second, then continues toward the entrance. "Come on. We aren't suspicious, not even a little bit."

"But if we're stopped, our IDs look nothing like us." I stand still, afraid to move just yet.

"If we can make it past the Reapers, we can make it past anyone." His words are confident, but his voice has a slight quiver.

I force my legs forward, following Exodus until we make it to the two large, heavy doors.

When did he become the voice of reason? Somehow, the sarcastic, white-haired inmate from Salem was now my best friend and source of logic.

He reaches out, gripping one of the handles. "Just stay calm."

I nod. In the newly created gap between the doors, a gust of frigid wind rushes through. My eyes instinctually shut.

The snowfall has died down a bit, but the breeze is stronger than ever.

The two of us step out into the night. I tilt my head. Both Reapers and their dogs are missing from the gate, and since the wind has been throwing the powder around, there aren't any footprints visible either.

"Well, I guess that makes things easier, huh?" Exodus strides out further, the only source of light being the spotlights atop the fortress.

I follow, tightly gripping my pistol in my left hand. "Maybe just a little."

Where did they go? They never just up and leave, especially without replacements.

I gaze up at the building across the street, and even though I can't see him, I'm positive Raphael has his sights on us. It lessens the edge.

Exodus and I head for the gate. The doors behind us open as we're about to pass.

"Good evening, gentlemen," a woman says from behind. Her voice exudes mockery.

I don't know what spooks me more, the sudden noise, or the woman's voice.

The two of us cautiously turn around.

My mind breaks under a barrage of questions.

The tall woman is flanked by two men on either side of her. She wears a black leather trench coat, gray camo pants, black combat boots, and a black turtleneck.

Just like Matthew.

The men by her side wear gray sweatpants and black hoodies along with black morph masks—almost like a lazy interpretation of the Lazarus uniform.

I don't know what to do. Women aren't allowed to be soldiers, let alone Elite captains. . . Who is she?

A smile stretches too wide across her face. It emphasizes an unnatural expression. Her broad brown eyes are filled with hatred, her auburn hair is short and curly, and her pointy ears are overexaggerated for her face. The longer I stare, the more my sanity dwindles. *Am I hallucinating?*

"What?" She steps closer with her two men. "Cat got your tongue?"

My adrenaline spikes. "Uh, no ma'am."

Her smile twists into an overexaggerated frown, "You know, for someone who's trying to project himself as a Saint, you aren't doing a very good job, Jason."

The use of my name is painful. "What? That's not my—"

"*Quiet!*" she screams. The sudden burst almost makes me flinch. "You're the one who's trying to kill him! The one who slit his warm, perfect throat!"

Exodus's fingers twitch to his holster. "You're insane."

"Insane?" Her animalistic eyes go back and forth between us. "No, no I'm not insane. I'm a product of God, a product of perfection." She focuses on me. "I've had such a fun time with your lovely lady. I've loved every scream she's let out, every drop of blood she's shed. Her open wounds taste sweet, almost like raspberries."

My face twists into a grimace. I aim my gun at her, but her speed is unreal as she covers the distance between the two of us in a heartbeat. I try to squeeze the trigger, but she's already in my face, pulling her own gun from inside her trench coat and forcing the barrel up to my head, "I'll violate her again, and again, and again! I'll make you watch as I cut out her tongue and feed it to—"

My entire body locks as a gunshot explodes, but it isn't caused by her. The left side of her head bursts into a gory mess. Skull, brains, and teeth fly into the air, painting the visible parts of my face black.

I hastily step back, and in sync Exodus and I sway of our guns and fire multiple bullets into each of the men's heads. They collapse. Blood seeps out of their masks and paints the white around them scarlet.

I take the back of my hand and wipe black spatter from my mouth, spitting the excess into the snow.

I move my legs, but an evil sight unfolds right in front of me.

The woman's torso jerks upright. She gets to her feet. A black liquid spews from her gaping face and morphs into a shape that resembles the parts that were lost. Something Rebirth could never do.

Exodus swears, putting three rounds in her stomach.

She stumbles a bit, but black ooze peeks out of her fresh wounds and clots them instantly.

Her two men also get to their feet, both laughing. One of them reaches for the holster attached to his thigh.

I aim my gun at him and fire twice. One bullet hits his neck, and the other, his sternum. He flinches but fails to fall. He barrels toward me, throwing a punch.

I dodge, grabbing his arm to break it.

He swings the other arm. His knuckles break against my jaw.

I let go. He knees me in the gut, hits me in the face once more, and reaches for the knife attached to my tactical belt. I swat his hand away, lunging forward and biting into his neck.

Blood gushes into my mouth, but he doesn't seem fazed, and he is ripped away from me and tackled to the ground by Exodus, who takes his unsheathed knife and jams it into the man's covered face.

The other masked stranger is helping the woman stay

balanced. Her face begins to look. . . normal. Parts of the black ooze fade to a paler color. One of her eyes has fully returned. It glares at me with a hatred I can't even describe.

The urge to puke builds in my throat. My mouth fills with saliva. I stumble back a few feet, ice flowing through my veins.

Another booming gunshot echoes out. The woman takes another devastating blow to her partially reconstructed face.

Her body falls to the ground.

The man by her side looks up at the building across from the fortress, and a third shot fires off, sending him to the snow next to his master.

My thoughts scatter in different directions.

"Just die!" Exodus blurts.

His words snap me out of it. He again hurls the knife into the first stranger's face. I step over, cringing at the bloody mess. He's mutilated, but still grabbing at Exodus's throat.

He must be able to still see because his head abruptly tilts my way. "You can't kill us. You can't kill *you*."

I reel at his voice. A shockwave moves through me.

I point my pistol at his destroyed face and empty my mag into it. Wind spreads the gore all around us.

The thing on the floor goes limp. The more I gaze, the more I see the resemblance. The shoulders, the neck, the height, the sound of the voice.

I glance over at the woman. She's still lying in the snow with the other masked monster.

Her face is reconstructing, again.

Exodus and I exchange looks, reading each other's minds.

Run.

We sprint to Raphael. The snow slows us down, but not by much due to all the conditioning we were put through back when we had a base.

"Jason?"

"What?"

"He sounded just like you. . ."

We run in silence.

I glance to make sure we aren't being chased. Chewing the inside of my check, I respond, "I know."

CHAPTER THREE

The pink neon sign keeps flashing. The snow obscures some of the colorful blasts.

Raphael shuts the blinds. His face projects a wide array of emotions all at once.

The motel room is small, but in a weird sense, it's cozy. The walls are thin, so the howling wind is especially noticeable. The room is furnished with a small tv on an old desk and a mounted clock that ticks every second that passes. This is our hideout for now.

I sit on the edge of the only bed in the room. It creaks whenever I bounce my knee.

"How?" Raphael asks, pacing around the room. "How did they do that?"

"Do what?" Exodus takes a seat in a rickety chair.

"Immortality. I shot that woman, and she got right back up without half her friggin' head."

I remain silent.

"It must be a new thing." His pace hastens. "There's no way they had this ability before Christmas and didn't use it to defend

The God Code facility. Vice and I would have known about it if they did."

Exodus taps his finger on the nightstand beside him. "While we were inside Fenway, we came across this room where they had this naked chick tied down." He takes a deep breath. "You know how when you shot that freak outside, all this black crap came spewing out?"

"Yeah?"

"Well, these two dudes injected this naked girl with something that made her cry the same thing."

I take a deep, long breath. "There was also this white board in the torture room that had all these crazy writings on it. Whoever wrote it wanted Mills to. . . I dunno, I guess get her knocked up. . . It also mentioned how he's God and how I have to die. Since that crazy immortal chick was the only girl we saw—well, besides the one who was tied down and getting tortured—I'm gonna go out on a limb and say it's her. I mean, she was rambling on about how I'm the one who slit Mills' *perfect* throat, and how she's a product of God, so it kinda checks out."

Raphael shakes his head. "I'm so confused. Mills has never, and I mean *never* allowed a woman to hold authority, so why now?"

"Maybe his inner feminist has finally broke free?" Exodus mutters.

"Not the time," Raphael snaps.

"Sorry. Just trying to ease the tension."

My knee bounces faster. "There's something else we haven't told you."

"Which is?" Raphael crosses his arms.

"There were also writings on the white board talking about something called the *Maiden's Touch*."

"The Maiden's Touch?" He locks eyes with me. "The hell is that?"

"I don't know, it just said that it would be the end before the beginning."

He stops pacing. His eye widens. "They have *another* weapon of mass destruction?'

Exodus gazes down at the floor. "We don't know that."

He turns to me. "Why else would it be *the end before the beginning*?"

"I. . . I don't know."

"And they've made immortality possible—"

"She could just be one of a kind."

"I doubt it. . . If you and Blaine saw that woman crying the same black liquid, I'd be willing to bet that they took Rebirth and put it on crack." His voice raises an octave.

"It's okay, calm down—"

"Calm down? There may be another version of The God Code out there, and we haven't heard from Dante in over a month. Frye is still gone, and if Dante is dead, that means there's only three of us."

My heart grows heavy. His words have a bitter sting. I see Chloe in my mind. I see her on the dock with me in Seattle. We had won. Shutting down the God Code was supposed to be the second to last step.

Oh, how wrong I was.

What if I would've gone with her? Or maybe connected the dots that Raph would be at the rendezvous spot, and not at the pier?

Thinking of the pier, my heart tears for Kennedy. I barely knew the guy, but I know he looked up to me. He spent his last moments thinking I betrayed him. Flashes of his dead body bobbing up and down in the restless water plague my mind.

I blink them away.

The person who killed Kennedy was me. . . well, a Brenix that resembled me. I remember Marcy telling me about them back when I first rose from the dead. They mimic a person's appearance, attitude, and much more. They're exoskeletons covered in flesh and blood. They truly resemble human beings.

And there's two out here mimicking me and Raphael. We ran into them tonight.

"Okay." I stand from the bed and head over to the small bathroom. "So, let's just assume it is another weapon of mass destruction. What now?"

I immediately turn the sink on and watch as cold water pours from the faucet. I fill my palm then bring it to my lips. It tastes like sewage.

"We need to get a hold of Dante," Raphael replies. "And we need more people on our side."

"We need to find Chloe first," I argue, splashing my face with some of the water. "That has been our number one priority since the night she was taken."

"Jason, we've tried. We've done everything to find her, and every time we get a lead, they move her, or we get thrown off trail."

"Who knows how much longer we have before they kill her, we have to—"

"No, we don't have to do anything," Raphael snaps.

"She's probably still at Fenway right now. We could go back and get her out."

"And face that immortal again? Does that sound wise to you?"

"She's one of us. We wouldn't leave you if you were taken. In fact, if my memory serves me right, Tommy and I had to save your mangled ass from dying in Jersey."

"That's different." Raphael turns his back to me.

"How?"

"Because I actually—"

"You actually what? Huh?"

Exodus stands. "Guys, calm down, we can—"

"Shut your mouth, Blaine," Raphael mutters. He marches to me and jabs a finger in my chest. "You have no idea how long I've been fighting. Everything I've ever done was so that I could murder Mills and bring this nation back to its feet, but it's one thing after another, and I can't catch a break. We've spent the last two months searching for Frye, and it just isn't working."

A burning chest accompanies the grinding of my teeth. "How long you've been fighting? I was thrown into this against my will. I didn't ask to be executed, I didn't ask to be brought back, and I sure as hell didn't ask to be put through this much suffering. She's my last chance at something normal."

"Normal? Are you kidding me? Nothing in this world is normal. Look around you, we live in a society where a narcissistic psychopath who thinks he's God rules over all of us. You're eighteen years old and you've killed how many people? You don't get to live a normal life."

"You don't get to tell me what I can and can't do. You don't decide what I get to have." My vision blurs. I glance at the ceiling to prevent tears trailing down my flushed cheeks.

"You sound like a little girl dreaming for her Prince Charming, you know that? She isn't the only girl who can complete you. When will you stop being so reckless? The reason why death follows you wherever you go is because of all the stupid mistakes you keep making."

My hands ball into fists. "Name one."

"If you didn't stab that needle into Matthew the night we killed him, Simon would still be here. Bleach would still be here. Tommy would still be here. *Vice* would still be here. That one stupid mistake killed everyone you and I have ever cared about. If Matthew stayed dead that night, the task force would've been assigned to someone else, someone less vengeful. Your lust for getting equal with that maniac is what brought us here. You're the reason they're all dead. You're the reason Chloe is going to be tortured—"

My knuckles skid across his face. He stumbles back. I swing again, but he knees me in the gut and backhands me.

My teeth dig into my bottom lip. I taste blood. Grabbing him by the collar, I slam him against the wall.

He spits in my face, punching me in the side of the head.

Exodus rips me away and throws me onto the bed. "Yeah, let's add *more* crap to our list of problems! Let's just *kill* each other so Mills can go on vacation! Doesn't that sound fun, you two?"

Raphael glares at me. "You're a horrible heir. Everything you touch ends up dying. You're going to bury me and Blaine, you're going bury your girl, and then, one day, someone's going to bury you."

Fury rains over me. "*Go to hell!*"

Lunging, I take him to the floor.

He wraps his hands around my neck.

I thrash free and crush his nose with my forehead.

Before I know it, I'm reaching for my gun.

Exodus kicks the side of my face.

Stars appear everywhere. I fall to the side.

"What are you doing!" he yells. "You think this is solving anything? Look at yourself, man!"

I finally look at Raphael. Blood trails from his nose.

My emotions contradict one another. Which do I feel? Guilt or rage?

I get to my feet, throwing my hood over my head.

Raphael pinches his nose shut. "Where are you going?"

I ignore him, motioning Exodus my way. "Come on, I'm going to show you something."

"Show me what?" he questions.

"Memories."

"You can't leave," Raphael mutters. "It's past curfew. We're supposed to be keeping a low profile."

I readjust my hoodie, pulling the bottom over my holster.

Exodus sighs. He looks down at our *leader*. "I'm gonna go calm him down."

He grunts, shaking his head, "This is exactly what I'm talking about. Reckless."

"Holy hell, you both are hot heads. Shut up, sit down, and chill out."

I step out into the cold.

Exodus follows me and shuts the door behind him, "What was that?"

"What was what?" I answer, refusing to meet his gaze.

"You went for your gun. What's wrong with you?"

I grit my teeth. "He blamed me for their deaths. . . I got carried away."

"You're lucky he didn't see it."

"You gonna tell him?"

"No."

"Then let's just move on."

"I need you to be honest with me."

"About?"

"Would you have actually done it?"

I remember when I first met Raphael. It was an eternity ago in an alleyway. He murdered some thug who was stomping my face. I thought he was going to be my savior, but he was just there to execute me. Somehow, even with Chloe stabbing him in the neck, me fighting him in the cemetery, and all the other crap that went down, we became brothers. Partners until the end.

More guilt settles into my stomach.

"No." I shove my hands into my pockets. "I would never."

I debate going back inside and begging for forgiveness, but Exodus reads my thoughts, "Give Raphael some time. You mentioned memories. What did you want to show me?"

I compose myself, quickly rubbing my eyes to cover up any emotion. "Where I was killed a year ago."

CHAPTER FOUR

Sneaking past checkpoints is easy, so getting to my old neighborhood doesn't take long. It's around midnight when we approach the abandoned checkpoint that Tommy once worked at.

Exodus reads the black and white sign atop the booth, "Brookhaven Estates, huh?"

Stepping closer, a chuckle escapes my mouth, "Yep, home to the coolest kids around."

He snorts, "Oh, for sure."

I approach the red and white security gate and throw one leg over. My blood freezes at the overwhelming sense of familiarity. I stop moving. I was murdered here about a year ago. So much has happened since. What if Raph's right? What if all of this is my fault? I already second guess myself enough as it is, so hearing it from someone else has thrown my thoughts in a frenzy.

Flashes of Simon on his knees blind me. The smog in the air, the tension that could be cut with a knife. The sound of him choking on the blood that had pooled from his slashed esophagus.

None of that would have happened if I had let Matthew stay

dead. Why did I bring him back? Why was getting equal so important to me? Wasn't killing him enough?

In the spur of the moment, I guess I told myself he was a nobody, and that getting brought back to life after being murdered would only put him in a twisted shell of his former self. Instead, revenge fueled his existence.

It gave him a reason to live.

I stand where my dad was killed. I remember his last words to me, "Jason, don't loo—." He was cut off by a bullet to the head.

"You good, man?" Exodus asks.

Blood runs from my eyes. I chuckle again, "Life's cruel."

"I know."

"Come on, I'll show you where I used to live."

We walk past the scene of my death. The houses on either side of us are completely abandoned and devoid of human life. We pass Julie's old house, then Simon's.

"The Pinder's," Exodus reads off the welcome mat as I reach for the doorknob.

It's locked.

"Step back," I tell him.

I kick underneath the knob, breaking the latch. The door swings open.

"Geez, man," Exodus stammers. "We could've gotten in through a window, you know?"

I don't say anything. It still smells the same. I immediately head for the stairs, and Exodus follows. He trips on one of the steps but catches his balance. We enter my room, and I sigh.

I haven't slept on a bed in months since Raphael won the game of rock, paper, scissors at the motel.

I take a seat on my old comforter, eyeing an old school uniform of mine on the floor. Reddish-brown stains cover the blue polo and brown khakis conjure memories of my fight with Jakob.

It's funny. I wish that was all I had to deal with. I miss living a life where all I had to worry about were my grades, a couple of douchebags, and an underlying feeling of impending doom. Sure, there were cameras everywhere, bloodthirsty Saints who were itching to kill, and loads of propaganda, but I had some form of innocence. Some form of naivety.

Maybe naivety is the wrong word. I was willfully ignorant.

I'm sure I could have found Chloe. She lived in Collingsworth, but maybe one day her and I would have bumped into each other. Maybe at a restaurant? We'd fall in love. I'd show her off to everyone. I'd get on one knee and pop the question. My mom would cry. She always thought marriage was the most important thing, and I'm starting to agree. Cliché as it may sound, love is the strongest bond. I used to believe it was hate, but when I think of Chloe, she takes priority.

I've murdered people for that woman.

"What are you thinking about?" Exodus dispels my thoughts.

"Just things. . . it's weird being back in my old room. It makes me feel ordinary again."

"Good for you." Exodus glances around. "Smells like angsty teen in here, though."

I smirk, "I was never angsty."

"You definitely are now, Sir Edge-lord."

"You're way edgier than I am."

"You're kidding me, right?"

"You inherited your dead dad's prison sentence and grew up in Salem."

"Okay? You were murdered and brought back to life to serve a terrorist organization whose purpose is to assassinate the president."

Fair point.

"Okay. . . well, you have albinism," I counter.

He laughs, "How is that edgy? Also, I'm Italian, I was already white to begin with—and it could be worse, I could have those weird twitchy eyes."

"You wear sunglasses in the day. See? Edgy."

"You got a Saint's daughter killed."

"Ah, too soon." A twinge of regret tugs at my heart.

"My bad."

He sits down next to me. There's still a bottle of pills on my nightstand. Again, I think of the day Jakob got his hand sawed off by a Saint.

It makes me smile. Watching a blade tear through his wrist was sheer bliss.

Exodus exhales, "Let's talk about Chloe."

My heart drops. "What? You gonna tell me to give her up like Raphael did?"

"No, not at all. Raph didn't need to say that. He was out of line."

"Then what? Why ask about her?"

"We can't just leave her, you're right. But what do we do now?"

"That's the million-dollar question. I have no idea."

"Think she's still in Fenway?" Exodus leans against the door frame.

"Probably, but with that psychotic whore scouting around, we're as good as dead if we go back." I fall back on the mattress and stare at the ceiling.

"True, but there has to be a way. I know I came into the picture way later, but she stills means a lot to me. She's cunning, sweet, and not to mention deadly."

"Wish Raph could see that."

"He's just stressed, man. Whenever we take a step closer to winning, Mills hurls us back three. We thwart one doomsday attempt, and boom. He just plots another. We keep getting picked off one by one, and there's barely anyone left. I think he's just scared of losing you or me if we keep going after her."

His words induce a sigh, "I know that, but I also know that he cares about her, too. So why is he so willing to just leave her behind? Why does he want us to move on so badly when she's been with us since the beginning? I know he doesn't want to lose us, but he's okay with losing her?"

"I see what you mean."

We're sit in silence for a moment.

Footsteps interrupt our brooding.

Someone's walking around downstairs.

I sit up, eyes fixed on the closed door. Exodus doesn't move a muscle.

Not just one pair of steps. Two.

"Come on, we've gotta hide," Exodus whispers, shifting toward the closet.

I step off the bed. The springs groan, and the entire house goes quiet.

My breathing sinks deep into my chest. "Don't move."

The two of us stay completely still, the disturbance lying silent.

Rapid footsteps stammer up the stairs.

Exodus swears, reaching for his gun.

I go for mine too, but the door flies open, and the two androids mimicking me and Raphael enter.

"We knew you would be here." my mimic charges me, his face still disfigured from our earlier encounter.

I pull my gun from its holster, but he slams me down on the bed, causing my finger to jam into the trigger.

A bullet flies into the ceiling. My mimic wraps both hands around my throat.

"I know everything about you. My synthetic brain is filled with your thoughts, desires, and fears."

I stab my gun into his side and shoot twice. Artificial red sprays from his rib cage. He doesn't flinch. He doesn't even feel it.

My throat burns. The force is crushing my windpipe.

Dying. Death. Burning. Help. Help.

My mimic tilts his head. His blue eyes, identical to mine, bore into me. "Aw... you're in emotional distress."

I shove my barrel into the fresh hole in his body, pushing and jostling it in as far as I can. With a wheeze, *"I'll kill you!"*

"Unlikely."

I fire twice more, one of the shots sending him into a quick tick. He loosens his grip on me. I twist his left wrist until it snaps, escaping from under his grasp and throwing him against my nightstand.

Exodus is pushed up against a wall, Raphael's mimic poised to slit his throat.

I grab the back of his hoodie and pry him away, battering my foot against his kneecap. He buckles to the floor, swiftly thrusting a knife my way.

I lurch back into my mimic. We slam into another wall.

My gun falls to the floor.

"Watch out!" Exodus shouts.

I turn.

My mimic thrusts a hidden blade.

I swat his hand just in time.

He shoves me toward my door. I try to regain my balance, but he lunges, and the two of us break through the oak entrance.

We exchange fists, battling down the hallway. He throws me into a lamp, and I punch him in the face.

He headbutts the bridge of my nose.

"I know how you fight." His fist connects with my jaw.

I growl, grabbing him by the arm and hurling him at my parent's bedroom door. The force is so strong that he crashes through the door and falls to the floor.

I sprint toward him, grabbing a picture frame off my dad's old desk as I rush past. I leap on top of my doppelgänger as he attempts to get up. Rapidly and repeatedly slamming the corner of the frame into his face, blood gushes all over the carpet.

I shove the almost broken corner into his eye socket just as he thrusts his hips, making me stumble. I desperately fight but fail to remain on top of him.

He jumps to his feet and grabs my hood.

A burst of profanity escapes my lips as he drags me across the room and through the hall. I struggle with everything I've got, reaching for the knife I have sheathed through my belt loop.

I stab him in the stomach.

Unflinching, he lobs me down the stairs.

My body crashes against every other step until my back hits the wall at the bottom.

With pain and a spinning head, I manage to open my eyes just in time for his foot to slam against my face.

I feel for my knife. It's gone.

He pulls me to my feet, swinging his knuckles.

I dodge, and his fist leaves a hole in the wall.

I reach for my gun, which isn't there, and he slams into me a second time.

The front door is wide open. I move our fight into the snow.

The lack of porch lights leaves the snowy night extra dark. Electricity in the subdivision was shut down when everyone was killed.

I backstep over and over, increasing the distance between us,

He needs to charge again. That way I can dodge and cave his leg in.

"Come on!" Blood spills freely from my split lips

The thing's face is even more mangled than before. "You want me to rush in so that you can break my leg." He reaches into his back pocket. "It only slows me down for a little bit, you know?"

He pulls out a taser and shoots it at me.

The prongs puncture my skin. A surge of electricity drops me to my knees.

My mimic walks closer, still sending voltage. "Humans are ignorant. How many times has someone captured you and your partners, just for the bunch of you to escape? They give you so many opportunities to succeed, but not us. . . I know your every thought."

The electric flow ceases. I rip the prongs out and collapse face-first against the asphalt.

My lungs are desperate for air.

"Making a Brenix requires a lot of data," he continues. "Throughout history, the government has used them for the purpose of safety. A bureaucrat is scared that an insurrectionist wants to take his life while attending a meeting, so he sends in a Brenix to attend in his place while he listens in." He tosses the taser to the ground. "While you and your friends were being tortured inside the Estate, my handlers gathered plenty of data and inputted me with it. They took samples of your blood, spit, sweat, tissue, hair and dissected the data from it. While you were under the influence of intense psychotropic drugs, they took scans of your brain, and were able to retrieve the core of your persona and give it to me. Inside my fake mind, I lived the same childhood, and the same death. I understand why you feel the way that you do, and that's why killing you is too easy."

Bloody drool leaves my lips. My muscles are too weak to prop me up.

A commotion breaks out from my house. Exodus is thrown through a window next to the front door. He slams against the cement, and Raphael's mimic jumps out after him, grabbing and dragging his thrashing body across the lawn.

"Immobilize him," my mimic orders.

I shy away as the other stomps Exodus into submission.

He's then thrown next to me.

The both of us lie still, defeated.

Raphael's mimic pulls a gun and aims it at us while the other fishes into his pocket and takes out a smartphone.

"Look at me," he demands.

The two of us don't move.

"Fine. I'll just let her do the talking."

Her voice wakes me up.

"J-Jason. . .?"

My head lifts, finding the phone screen. It's a video chat. Her green eyes are filled with tears.

"Chloe?" In a flash, I'm ready for round two. "Is that really you?"

"Yes, yes I'm here. What's happening?"

My mimic smiles, "We want to crush all your hopes and dreams. Robyn's orders."

He takes the other mimic's gun and points it at my face.

She gasps, "Wait, no, no, don't—"

Suddenly, both mimics are slammed with a battery of bullets. Their bodies thrash under the assault, and the real Raphael appears from the darkness with a blazing barrel in hand. The two clones fall to the ground, but he doesn't stop. He puts multiple holes in each of their heads as he gets closer and closer. Eventually running out of ammo, he stomps my mimic's skull, not relenting until there's exposed wires and gore. He repeats this to his own, and after what feels like an eternity, he slings his weapon over his shoulder, apparently satisfied with the outcome of his effort.

Adrenaline gives me enough energy to kneel. "What are you doing here?"

"Aren't you happy to see me?" He reaches his hand out.

I grab it and allow him to pull me to my feet.

Exodus gets up on his own, "Happy? Nah, we *wanted* to take a couple bullets to the face. Thanks, man."

"I didn't like how we left things, and I wanted to talk," Raph shrugs. "You mentioned memories, so this is the first place I looked."

"Thanks for not being a pompous dickhead." Exodus pulls a piece of glass out of his forearm.

"Pompous? You an old lady, or something?"

I ignore them, scrambling for the phone my mimic dropped. I pick it up, and bliss swims through my veins when I see her. She's crying, but there's a little smile on her face.

"Where are you?" I don't waste any time.

"I don't know. A Saint just came in, set a phone up in front of me, then left. They moved me about an hour ago from the old ballpark back home."

"I know. We were just there."

"You were?"

"We've been looking for you since the night you were taken." My vision turns red. "I thought I was never going to find you."

Raphael grabs the phone from my hand. "Be gushy later. Describe the room you're in."

She hesitates, "It's big and dark. There's a little light bulb hanging from the ceiling above me, but that's my only lighting."

"To confirm, they took you out of Fenway?"

"Yeah, I only got here about twenty minutes ago."

"By car?"

"Yeah."

"Okay, so you're still in Boston. . ." he pauses for a moment. "That still leaves too many possibilities."

"They're going to publicly execute me in twenty days. Their plan is to tell everyone that I'm one of the Lazarus members responsible for making and setting off the God Code. I thought we sent off a broadcast putting all the blame on Mills?"

"We planned on it," Exodus chimes in. "But it didn't work out."

Raphael smirks, "You said a public execution? Where at? Do you know?"

"At the State House, downtown."

"What time?"

"I don't know."

"That's okay, we'll set up the night before."

"What are you three doofuses going to do?"

"Kill everybody and get you out of there."

She smiles, "Can't lie. . . I really thought you three were gonna leave me."

His smile fades. I know he feels guilty. "No, we would never leave you, Frye."

A sudden noise on her side startles her. "They're coming. Look, you need to know something. There's another doomsday weapon called—"

"The Maiden's Touch," Exodus mutters.

"Yeah. I've overheard so much. I'll tell you everything when you get me. Watch out for a woman—her name is Robyn—"

"Time's up, girly!" A deep voice shouts.

So, Robyn's the immortal.

Raphael throws the phone to the ground and smashes it.

"You're not keeping it?" Exodus asks.

"There's definitely some good information on it, but it also has a tracker."

A feeling hatches within me, allaying some of the fear that is like a solid mass in my gut. I thought she was gone. I thought they were going to torture her to death while I desperately tried to save her.

The feeling grows more. I resist the urge to cry.

I'm alive again.

The walkie-talkie attached to Raphael's waist crackles. Our eyes dart to it.

"Ramirez, do you copy?"

Raphael practically rips the radio from his belt. "Briggens? Yeah, I copy."

We wait. Then he replies, "I'm back."

CHAPTER FIVE

His trench coat sways in the wind. A prosthetic hand and a black metallic mask give him an ominous presence. I've known Dante Briggens since I was a kid. Julie was one of my best friends, and so whenever Simon and I would go over to her house, we'd see him. He'd just be getting off work, and despite being so young, I could tell his days as a solider were never kind to him.

Raphael catches his breath from all the sprinting and climbing we had to do to get to the rendezvous, on top of this building downtown. "Where have you been?"

"Canada," his voice is slightly muffled courtesy of the mask he wears. We were given an identical one before the God Code raid. "We need to talk, and by that, I mean I need you to listen to me, and very carefully."

"What's going on?"

"Have you found Chloe?"

"I guess you could say so."

"In your search for her, have you three heard anything about the Maiden's Touch?"

We all nod.

"How much do you know?"

"That it's another doomsday weapon." My words are carried away in the diminishing wind. "We made it inside Fenway tonight, and there was mention of it on a chalkboard—"

"It's a genetic cleanser," Dante interrupts. "Mills wants to rid the nation's underdogs. If you're injected with the Touch, and you have any sort of mental or physical handicap, the weapon will quickly eat away at your brain and kill you."

Raphael stares, unfazed but annoyed nonetheless. "Why? Why does this prick keep playing God? Why is he so hellbent on killing his own people?"

"He isn't just *playing*; he's trying to *become*. In the past year, his sanity has eroded away. He's lost it. He's completely insane. We all thought he was bad before, but. . ."

Exodus clears his throat, "What happens to those that aren't genetically screwed?"

Dante sighs, "They are granted immortality. The Maiden's Touch is a product of reverse engineered Rebirth with its effects amplified ten-fold. Not only can they not be killed, but the Touch also prevents them from aging, getting diseases, and more."

I tense, "So Mills is going to let random people in his society become immortal? What happens when someone who loathes him becomes unstoppable?"

"He has a failsafe, but I haven't figured it out yet. There are rumors saying it's going to be some sort of device he will implant in each immortal. He's going to use the genetically pure as breeders, and after they've served their purpose, he's probably going to use that unknown weakness to kill them. He'll receive a new generation of *perfect* children who will look to him as a god because they won't know any different. He'll live on forever while they worship him. We, on the other hand, will be dead."

Raphael swears, "But. . . it's only been like two months. How have they put such an insane idea together in such little time? Let alone, engineer the weapon?"

Dante shakes his head. "This has been in the works for years. Mills was going to let a select few live and act as a group of breeders. He refers to them as Adams and Eves; he was going to weed out the weak-links with the Touch, then use the immortal survivors to create genetically pure children."

"Wait, so this isn't new? You've known about it?"

"I only knew a little bit. I knew about the God Code, and the Adams and Eves, but very little about the Maiden's Touch. Mills may have had a closer relationship with his Reapers, but he didn't tell us everything."

My jumbled thoughts are on a hamster wheel. "Why were you in Canada?"

"The whole point of me leaving you three was to recruit more members for Lazarus. Trying to recruit people here in the states would be a bad idea without more numbers to keep them in line and train them. So I went to a place where the population would be just as bloodthirsty and ready to kill Mills as we are."

"Um. . . care to elaborate?" I ask.

"Didn't you pay attention in school? After winning the war, Mills enslaved the remaining survivors and now uses them to mine, farm, and gather resources for us. Initially, all of Canada was completely wiped out, but since the resources there are so rich, it serves as a hotspot for all the enslaved. The Saints take detainees from all over the world and bring them to Canada, giving us a lot of candidates to choose from."

Raphael seems lost in thought, but suddenly speaks, "But clearly that didn't happen since you're here by yourself, so what went wrong?"

"We posed as slaves; wore the uniforms, did the hard, back breaking labor, outdid each requirement. I was in the process of talking to one of the more influential individuals when a bunch of soldiers stormed the mess hall and dragged random people away. I was informed by the others that those being taken were being experimented on. I dropped the whole recruitment scheme and gathered as much information as I could, which was already difficult since a large portion of the slaves only spoke broken English. They had a lack of education and were forbidden to speak their native tongue, so I did most of it by myself. It took weeks for me to find anything, and by the time I did, most of our undercover members were either dead or dragged away to become guinea pigs."

Raphael rubs his temples. "So what you're trying to tell me is that it's just us four?"

"With what I have put in place, you aren't going to need more than that."

"What do you mean?"

"I'm sure you three remember Cass."

I remember the brunette girl that helped me blow up the hospital. She was one of the two people I saved back at the Estate when her, Kennedy, Sam, and Ross were held at gunpoint. I try to forget ever having to make that decision. It's been a struggle to bury that memory since the night it happened.

I slowly nod. "Yeah, what about her?"

"I left her behind at one of the bigger facilities. She's posing as one of the cooks since the female slaves don't do manual labor. Let's just say kitchen duty is a blessing compared to the other jobs most girls are assigned to."

"Why'd you leave her?" Exodus asks.

"She has a mini camera embedded into her clothes along with a hand-cam hidden under her mattress. For the next little while, she's going to get footage of all the horrible things that happen under Mills' autarchy. She's going to capture footage of executions, people being treated as sub-human, and the disgusting things that they do to the women. During my investigation, I discovered a lab inside the camp where the taken slaves were brought to be experimented on. It's where I found everything out about the Maiden's Touch. They're injecting the slaves with it and monitoring them so that they can make tweaks where needed. Cass is going to stealth in and get it all on camera."

Raphael tilts his head. "What for? Why all the recording?"

"Once she's done, she's going to sneak on one of the computers in the lab and send us the footage. Then we try again. We tried but failed back in Seattle, but this time we'll broadcast Mills' insanity to every screen in the nation. People are already fed up with the death, so imagine the chaos once they know about the newest addition to Mills' doomsday arsenal. There will be riots in the streets. Saints being hunted down and killed by crowd. Government buildings will be raided, officials will be hanged, and while that's happening, we'll find Mills and put an end to his life."

Enthusiasm? The emotion is foreign as it flows through me. "You're right. . ."

Raphael grins, "You just love blowing me away. Don't you, Briggens?"

"You're a genius," Exodus says.

Dante sighs, "I just want my shot at Mills. Bastard's going to pay for what he did to me."

The grin fades from Raph's face. He takes a step closer to Dante. "You mentioned Chloe. I'll fill you in on what you've missed. In twenty days from now, she'll be executed at the State House. Best part? It'll most likely be by Mills. That psycho would never let anyone else get recognition for killing a member of Lazarus."

Dante peers back, the rooftop serves as a perfect vantage point to see the State House. He gazes at the large red and bronze building. It looks vintage compared to the tall modernized business complexes and hotels surrounding it.

"He's probably going to behead her. My favorite," Dante says.

I chime in, "Don't get too excited. We're going to save her."

"And how do you propose we do that?" he asks.

Raphael smirks, "We're a smart bunch, aren't we? We'll figure it out."

Exodus yawns with a stretch.

Dante and Raphael descend the ladder leading to the fire escape. Exodus and I share a glance, then follow.

Time to plan a raid.

CHAPTER SIX

The days leading to the execution drag on. Raphael and Dante are both plan freaks, so the two of them spend most of their time plotting and getting all the supplies needed while Exodus and I sit inside the motel and die of boredom. The only thing on tv is propaganda and old horror films. Exodus tries to learn card tricks with a deck he stole from a corner store, and I think while Dracula, The Wolf Man, and Frankenstein stalk their prey in the background. This repeats, over and over. Day in, and day out.

Thoughts are deadly when one is alone. I over analyze everything, and an abundance of unnecessary questions plague my mind. Chloe was put through Rewired when Vice was still alive. Could Mills still use that? Or was it destroyed when Dante disabled the bombs inside our heads? What if it wasn't Chloe on the video chat? What if it was some sick trick to lure the remainder of us to our doom?

I picture the four of us in position, ready to save her, when someone puts a gun to my head and blasts my skull wide open. Mills would laugh like a madman.

After I lost Simon, the only thing that kept me going was

revenge. Even with that undying rage, I didn't truly care if I lived or died. I was so tired of pain and its constant companionship. It demanded to be felt, and I felt it more than anything. I thought when I killed Matthew, I served my purpose, but then Chloe was taken from me. Since that night, I've had a lot of time to realize just how much I love her and how much I want to be with her. Crave and desire. Two words that engulf me whenever I picture her beautiful face. She's pale like a vampire. Her eyes are the prettiest I've ever seen.

How can I not love her after everything that's happened. It would be almost impossible not to. She's been with me since the beginning. Since the escape from Lazarus, our capture and return, Fight-Night, Fort Alister, and Simon's death. She calms my frenzied mind, and despite all the hell we've been put through, when I see her, I'm home again.

I miss home.

Death scares me because I finally have a reason to live again. I have a chance to be happy.

It's gushy, but when I saw her on that phone screen, something ignited inside me.

Part of me fears being so attached. This route we're on is deadly. After rescuing her, it'll only be a matter of time before Cass has all the footage and the nation will be rioting. We also can't forget about Robyn, or the fact that she's immortal, and wants me to rot.

My chances of surviving have never been high. Is it bad that I want out? That I want to run away with Chloe and try to discover normality with her? What about Raphael and the others? What would they do without us? Would I be betraying them?

I slip my hoodie over my wet hair and exit the bathroom.

Raphael and Dante are gone, but Exodus sits on the bed. He's watching Dracula for the fifth time this week.

My presence grabs his attention.

"You were in there for like two hours," he chuckles. "Testosterone, huh?"

I laugh, "Nah, just some severe trauma that gets me trapped inside my head from time to time."

"That's pretty valid, but I still think—"

"You can think what you want, pervert."

We laugh some more. I sit in the chair near to the bed. "Aren't you getting tired of this black-and-white movie crap?" I lean back.

"Meh. It's better than hearing about how *loving* our *dear* President is. Didn't you hear? He wants us all to live long and happy lives."

I dramatically swoon, "Oh, my hero."

"You know, after this whole rebellion thing, you and I should be stand-up comedians."

"Oh, for sure." I look around the room once more. "So, where'd they run off to now?"

"It's almost curfew. They're waiting for the night to cover them so they can set up our little diversion for tomorrow."

"I'm so lost, man. I don't even know what they're planning."

He gets up and shuts the movie off. "Yeah, probably because they keep switching it up."

"What's the latest?"

"You'd think since you're the heir, you'd be filled in on this crap before I was, huh?"

"They probably told me. I've just been doing a lot of thinking," I retort.

Exodus opens the mini fridge in the kitchen and grabs a drink. "Last I heard, they're planting bombs in two rooms on each side of the main hall. They'll detonate when Chloe's about to die. Chaos ensues, I smoke the place out with chlorine gas, you save your pretty little lady, and yadda yadda ya."

"What if they don't care about the explosions and continue with the execution?"

"As always, Raph's going to be at a vantage point with a sniper rifle."

"How are we going to deploy the gas?"

"That's my job." He takes a sip of his drink. "In fact, I'm supposed to leave here in a minute to go set up the dispensers. It's gonna be wicked."

His words trigger events from earlier. "Oh yeah, I remember now. I'm going to be in the audience as a spectator, and there's going to be two gas masks taped to the bottom of my chair."

"Bingo, and once the gas goes off, you rush in, being her *heroic* prince, putting a mask over her face so she doesn't literally cough up a lung and die choking."

"What about the civilians in the crowd? Executions *always* have a crowd," I say. "We aren't going to kill a bunch of innocent people, are we?"

"No, it's just higher ups and their families, remember?"

"Their families?"

"They're evil people. Each and every one of them, dudezo."

"I know, but—"

"It's either this, or Chloe dies."

My jaw tenses. "Yeah. . . You're right."

"Dante went out and got you a suit for tomorrow. We're hiding out in a couple of closets tonight, that way we're already in and won't have to go through security. Once everyone flutters in, you step out, and *presto*. Hey, if we're lucky, you might even be able to get a lil' stabby stab at Mills. It'd be dope if you could slit his stupid throat again."

"How are we even getting inside? I'm sure security is tight, especially the night before something like this."

"Yeah, there's definitely security, but earlier today, Dante was able to get in and leave a window unlocked."

I sigh. My shoulders slump. "I'm really sorry I haven't had my head in this, man."

"No, I get it. What are you thinking about anyway?"

"I—" I contemplate a lie. "I've just been thinking about what happens after we kill Mills and everyone beneath him. What's going to happen next? Who's going to take charge?"

"Hell, if I know. Raphael for the time being?" He walks to the nightstand and picks up his deck of cards. "But hey, I know that isn't really what's on your mind."

"What?"

He shuffles the cards. "I was in Salem for a long time. Everyone I knew was either a criminal, or a Saint, and both have one thing in common."

"Which is?"

"They're both really good liars, and if you spend enough time around them, you can start to see through all the bull crap."

"So you think I'm lying?"

"Oh, I know you are."

The sound of him shuffling fills the silence.

I stare. The walls creak and groan from the wind outside. "I'm scared of dying."

He laughs, "Oh, for real? Hey, man. Same."

"You don't get it. I finally have a chance at happiness."

"With Chloe, yeah?"

My eyes lower. "Yeah."

"You'll be fine, dude." He shoves his cards back into a little container and slips it in his pocket. "Speaking of which, it's time to go save her."

I take a deep breath, standing from the chair. "Lead the way."

CHAPTER SEVEN

The entrance hall is ornately decorated. Twelve rows of chairs take up most of the space, but my attention is on the staircase twenty feet ahead. Five marbled steps lead to a landing where a lectern stands—on either side of the lectern, the staircase splits in two, leading to the open second story where more spectators watch from above.

Two of our nation's flags hang from the enormous ceiling. From the windows, the sun highlights the colors.

I take a seat in the second to front row. A black suit and red tie adorn my body.

I can't keep my leg from bouncing as I wait for the main event.

Chatter fills the venue, and no matter how much I try to ignore it, I can't stop myself from focusing on a group of kids grabbing food from a decorated appetizer table.

"Chill." Exodus's voice rings through an earpiece hidden by my messy hair. "Dante said he was going to try and get the kids out before the explosions or chlorine gas go off."

"How?" I ask, my tone hushed.

"Beats me but have some faith. While you and I played slap

jack in the janitor closet all night, he was planning for something like this."

"That last round was dirty, and you know it."

"Oh, shut up."

Dread ravages my chest. This is my last chance at saving her, and if anything goes wrong, she'll die.

Die... Die. Die. Die. Die. Die.

A woman with short, curly red hair approaches the lectern. She's wearing the Elite guard uniform, and her smile is stretched too wide.

Robyn.

She checks to see if the microphone is on before speaking. "Good morning, ladies and gentlemen." Everything about her face is unnatural. "I know that each of you are anticipating the President's speech, but we're just going through some last-minute safety protocols to ensure that everyone here remains safe and unharmed."

There's a small round of applause. I begrudgingly follow the crowd.

The skin around Robyn's lips split, "In the back, we have a camera crew that will be broadcasting this morning's event to every screen in America, so when our great and valiant leader is talking, please be silent. Everyone here is either an official beneath Mills, or related to one, so please be an example."

Everyone affirms. Our national anthem plays.

A door upstairs opens, and two Reapers appear. They march forward, and behind them, Mills appears with another duo of Reapers guarding from behind.

A roar of applause breaks out. My dread is replaced with rage.

He walks with his cane, even though he doesn't need it. I wonder if he's an immortal, just like Robyn. I contemplate the idea. The thought of being alone with him in a room and killing him over, and over again while he helplessly regenerates. The vivid picture stops my teeth from grinding.

Don't let your anger blow your cover. If he so much as spots you in the crowd, you're dead. Keep cool. You've gotta keep cool. It'll be over soon.

I take a couple deep breaths. Each exhale diminishes the flames that engulf my heart.

Mills approaches the lectern. His gray suit and purple tie don't hide his resonating arrogance.

His personal guards stand in a formation that blocks any access to him.

The crowd's applause dies down.

Mills rests his cane against the lectern, positioning the microphone an appropriate distance from his mouth. "Good morning, my dear friends. I'm so happy you could make it to this special occasion."

Exodus chimes in my ear, "Holy hell. He looks fifteen years younger than the last time we saw him."

"I know," I whisper. There isn't a scar on his throat from where I slashed it. "No scarring. He's definitely an immortal."

Mills places his hands on the lectern, expressionless. "Two months ago, our lovely city of Seattle was gassed by the terrorist organization known as Lazarus. The gas in question killed anybody who inhaled it, and it left hundreds of thousands of innocent civilians dead on the street while they desperately tried to evacuate." He pauses, looking past the crowd and into the cameras. "As I'm sure a lot of you have seen, I've started the construction of a great wall around the city. This is for security reasons that I won't be addressing at this time, but let's not forget to mention that this is all because of *them*. Isn't it quite ironic that the same organization who says they're trying to create a better America plans on doing so by gassing its inhabitants?"

You liar!

"I know everyone's hungry." His lips curl into a nasty grin stretched unnaturally wide. "So, before my personal chefs bring out their famous dishes, I am pleased to announce that we have captured one of the sub-humans in charge of engineering this weapon of mass destruction." Another door opens from upstairs. "You may recognize this *thing* from my Estate. After an attempt on my life, she escaped with the rest of her degenerate parasites. However, when you mercilessly kill my people, I will stop at nothing to find you. Ladies and gentlemen, this is the person who helped murder the men, women, and children of Seattle."

The tension in the air grows thick as Chloe is dragged down the stairs. She's wearing a bloody tank top and torn jeans. Her blond hair is matted in red.

The Reapers move in formation as Mills grabs his cane and steps away from the lectern and down the five steps. Chloe is dragged behind.

My earpiece goes off. "Keep calm."

My knuckles turn white. "I know."

Mills stands level to the crowd. Chloe is forced to her knees in front of him.

The Reapers stand guard, automatic rifles in hand.

Classical music plays overhead, and Robyn retrieves a portable microphone from behind the lectern and carries it to Mills.

He takes it, raising it to his mouth. "This sub-human's name is Chloe Frye. She works under the power and authority of Jason Pinder and Raphael Ramirez. She's killed for them, tortured for them." Mills hands the microphone back to Robyn, who holds it to his lips as he unsheathes the blade from within his cane. "So now, she must be put to death."

I grit my teeth. "How much longer?"

"I have no idea."

Time stands still. My lungs fill, then deflate. I put all my faith in Raphael and Dante.

Mills steps back, lying his sheathe down on the white marble floor next to his feet. "But before I put an end to her pathetic existence, I want to say hello to someone very important in the room." Mills looks directly at me. His evil smile stretches across his unnaturally white teeth. "Jason Pinder."

Before I can react, two additional Reapers from the back of the hall approach me, their weapons trained on the back of my head.

The crowd around me remains silent. A woman faints, and an overdramatic man hyperventilates.

Where were these idiots when I was in high school theatre?

I willingly stand and throw both hands in the air. Animosity reigns.

One of the Reapers bashes me in the face with the butt of his gun, sending me to my knees. He then grabs me by the arm and drags me out of the audience, taking me to the person who started this all.

Exodus's voice blares in my left ear. He's using every swear in the dictionary, telling me to hold on.

I know Raphael has his sights on me. He's viewing this from a well-planned vantage point, but if he shoots now, the Reapers will kill us all, and I'll have to face my fear.

Hundreds of people were surrounding me. How did he know? How did he know exactly where I was?

I'm thrown in front of him. His evil smile hasn't shifted.

"People of this great nation." Mills looks up at the cameras, still holding his sword. "Jason Pinder is one of the last remaining members of Lazarus. He's the one who slit my throat and murdered his way out of my Estate. He defiled the women who served me, committed abhorrent acts, did unspeakable things." He snarls. "He's Lucifer himself!"

My eyes find Chloe's. Despite the circumstance, she flashes a little smile. Time freezes, and I wonder if I'll ever be able to hold her again. Even on her knees with torn clothes and blood soaked hair, she has optimism and a look of hope.

I can't hear it, but I see her mouth, "Hey."

The music overhead reaches a crescendo. Mills raises his sword.

Exodus screams through the mic, *"Damn it! Where's the explosion!"*

"I won't show you any mercy!" Mills blurts. Spit flies from his mouth. "I am *God,* and you must now face your judgment!"

He swings his blade. I anticipate it, but a loud hiss stops him dead in his tracks.

Yellowish-green mist fills the room. The crowd panics.

"Don't breathe!" Exodus yells in my ear.

The room quickly fills with the poison. The crowd panics. The little kids cough and hack. One of them falls to the ground. Another man screams in agony, clawing at his throat.

"We have to evacuate you, my lord!" Robyn shouts, grabbing Mills by the arm.

He shoves her off. I dive out of the way just as his blade swipes at my neck.

Chloe kicks him in the leg. He stumbles back.

The Reapers aim their guns at us.

My ears explode as an eruption hits the room, causing debris to fly across the hall from both ends. The walls blast open. In unison, a gunshot goes off. The Reaper who pulled me from the audience gets his head split open, painting my new suit red.

More gunshots follow. Each Reaper falls to the floor.

The chlorine gas swallows me. I hold my breath, stammering to my feet and rushing toward my chair in the second row.

Gunfire breaks out upstairs. Hundreds of people drop to the floor around me and claw at their throats as they inhale the gas.

My eyes clamp shut. I reach my chair. I desperately feel underneath for the masks.

They're still there.

I rip the tape from them and hastily secure one to my face. My chest burns. I press a little button on the side of the mask, filtering out the gas and allowing me to breathe.

I still can't open my eyes, but I take the other mask and trip my way back to Chloe.

More shots echo throughout the building.

I press another button. This time, a tiny valve rinses my eyes with water. The sting fades and I open them, seeing Chloe amid the dead Reapers.

Her hands are over her mouth; her cheeks are turning purple.

I secure the mask to her face and press the filter and rinse buttons.

She inhales violently, choking and coughing as I help her to her feet.

I do a quick look around. Mills is gone. So is Robyn.

"Exodus." I pull out my gun and lead Chloe upstairs. "Are you already on the roof?"

"Yeah, you need to hurry."

"We're almost there."

We make our way through the sea of bodies collapsed on the floor.

One hand reaches up and grabs a hold of my leg. The man's eyes are bulging out of his skull. Two dead little girls lay next to him.

I cringe, pulling my trigger and putting him out of his misery.

The sight makes me sick.

"Jason," Chloe hacks, still by my side as I drag her along. "What's the plan?"

"A van is waiting at the edge of the property. Just stay with me."

We approach an open window. I climb through.

Exodus is sprinting across the tiles. Some of them break loose due to their age, tumbling off the roof.

We follow. More gunshots burst from the State House.

"Come on." Exodus stops at the edge of the roof, lowering himself. "We've gotta get down there, and we've gotta be quick."

We mimic his actions and climb down the building. My memory takes me back to Salem, especially to my fall. The way my broken body smacked against the grass chills me.

My grip tightens as we trapeze our way down to the lawn.

Our feet touch the snow-covered grass, and the gunshots

cease. The air grows completely still. Faint music still plays from inside.

At the edge of the property, Dante waits in a white van. He rolls down a window, "Where's Ramirez?"

"He's not with you?" I tug the side door open.

"No. Get in."

We comply and he slams his foot on the gas pedal, driving to the font of the building and parking in front of the wavy set of stairs that lead to the entrance.

Dante adjusts his earpiece. "Raphael, where are you?"

It's silent.

"Raphael?"

Again, nothing.

I peek my head up front, scrutinizing the building. Green gas seeps from beneath its doors.

Exodus swallows, "Here, I'll go get hi—"

The doors to the building fly open. Raphael and a Reaper fling from the entrance, exchanging bloody blows. The Reaper pries the gas mask from Raph's face and tosses it.

"There's our boy." My words force the rising bile back into my stomach.

"He needs to hurry. We only have a minute or two until backup arrives," Dante mutters.

Raphael grabs a knife from his belt, and after taking a swing to the gut, reels his arm back and jabs the blade through the Reaper's throat. The Elite grasps at his wound, collapsing onto Raphael who uses the momentum to throw him down the steps. The body twists and mangles all the way down.

Raph rushes toward us. He swings the passenger door open and jumps in. "Go!"

Dante slams his foot against the pedal.

As we flee down the street, sirens fill the air behind us.

CHAPTER EIGHT

I'm lighter. It's as if a weight has been taken off my chest. My thoughts are clearer. Energy returns to my steps. Every breath that enters my lungs fills me with vitality.

She's not dead. She's in the bathroom taking a shower.

I barely notice Exodus's meltdown over what just happened.

"Where was the explosion? Jason was about to take a sword to the neck. He could've *died*."

Dante stands near the window. The blinds are shut. He calmly answers, "There were snipers everywhere. What? Did you want your head to burst the second you left the building? I had to take them out."

Exodus turns to Raphael. "Why didn't you take a shot at Mills when he was swinging at Jason?"

"Why do you think? Could it be because, oh, I don't know, without the proper distraction they would have just gunned the two of them down once I took the shot?"

"But—"

I pull myself from my gleeful recovery. "It's okay—it might've been a bit sloppy, but we got what we came for."

Dante steps away from the window and enters the kitchen, "We were stupid for not putting you in some sort of disguise."

"Like what? It's not like he could've worn a mask. That would've drawn far more attention." Raphael sits at the foot of the bed. "Look, what happened was probably the best result we could've hoped for."

Exodus shakes his head, snorting, "Yeah, because who wouldn't hope for a bunch of dead kids?"

A growl emits from Dante's throat, "Don't put that on me. I tried."

Exodus stands from the chair. "You know what probably would've helped? *Communication*. Neither of you said a damn word the entire time."

Raphael also stands. "I was laying down on a rafter just above two Reapers. Did you expect me to have a full-fledged conversation with you? Maybe tell you about my unresolved childhood trauma?"

"Screw you."

"Will you guys shut up?" I mutter. "There's six of us left, one in Canada. Instead of fighting like a bunch of children, let's plan out our next move."

"I agree." Dante grabs a paper towel. He uses it to wipe away some of the drying blood on his forehead. "I think our first course of action is finding a real base of operations, where we can store supplies."

"Anywhere come to mind?" Raphael asks.

Dante shrugs, "Not really, unless Lazarus has any more of those secret facilities hidden about the nation?"

Raph tucks his chin. "Matthew destroyed all of them. The one in Jersey was the last. Thanks to that prick, it's also gone."

Exodus rubs his covered forearm. "What about that one place you were talkin' about way back? The hotel Vice used for stuff. The Sweet Spider?"

"We're not using The Sweet Spider."

"Why not?"

"Vice is dead. It's not under our control anymore. It'd be pointless."

I speak up, "What's wrong with where we're at now?"

Dante heaves out an emotionless chuckle, "This place is the definition of small. We aren't gonna be able to store anything here. Plus I don't think it is fair that only one of us gets a bed. We need a new place where no one will find us and where we can fortify and store weapons."

"Exactly," Raphael says. "An abandoned school building would do the trick, and believe it or not, there isn't a lack of them around."

The door to the bathroom opens. Chloe steals my attention as she steps into view. Her wet blond hair has grown out a bit. It gracefully frames her pale face and green eyes.

She's wearing the clothes Exodus and I stole for her: a black hoodie that's a size too big, dark blue jeans, and white sneakers.

She smiles, which turns into a little laugh, "This place is trashy."

My heart sings.

Exodus pulls out his deck of cards, "You try finding a place to lay low when the entire government is trying to hunt you down."

Her smile gradually fades. "Yeah. Yeah, I know."

My thoughts from yesterday push to the forefront of my mind, and without thinking, I ask, "Hey, can we talk outside?"

Her eyes meet mine. "We could do that."

Exodus smirks, "Don't forget that teenage pregnancy—"

"Will you quit with that?" Raphael interrupts. "Seriously, it's the most annoying thing in the world."

Chloe and I exit the motel, stepping out into the cool afternoon air. People rushing home after a long day of work fills the air with a droning hum, and since the winter forces the sun to set early, I'm forced to squint at the unwelcomed rays.

The icicles hanging from the motel's gutters drip out an unrhythmic melody.

We stare at each other, allowing the drips and traffic to fill the silence. There's so much I want to say, so many unfinished thoughts and desires I want to share. She's been gone forever, and despite dreaming about this exact moment for weeks, I can't decide where to start.

"I thought you were gone," I eventually squeak out. Our gaze still unified.

She embraces me, wrapping her arms around my shoulders and resting her head against my chest.

I breathe, allowing my posture to relax.

"I missed you, too," she whispers.

She doesn't let go. I rest my cheek atop her head. Her blond hair tickles my nose.

A soothing wave breaks over me.

"I love you," she says.

My heart flutters, "You what?"

She looks up, red tracing down her cheeks. "I love you so much. You didn't give up on me. . ."

My fears rush up my throat. I try to stop the words from escaping my lips, but it's too late.

"Let's run from here."

"What?"

"Let's leave, run away somewhere safe. Be together."

Scarlet continues to trace down her pale cheeks. "But what about Lazarus?"

Guilt punches me in the gut. "They have a plan. Cass is at a slave camp in Canada, and she's getting footage of everything for us to leak to the nation. Once everyone sees what the Maiden's Touch is, they'll riot. It'll be the last straw. They've got this. We can go."

"Go. . .? That sounds peaceful."

"I know, and we can do it, right now."

"I can't."

"Why?"

"Jason. The idea of running away together sounds wonderful, and I want it—"

"Then have it."

"But after what they did to me, to my family. . . I can't just walk away."

"But Chloe—"

"She wasn't allowed to kill me. She did everything but that, and I mean *everything*. I can still hear her laugh. Feel her tongue on my face—"

"Who's *her*? Robyn?"

"Yeah, and I'm really sorry, but I can't leave until she's dead."

"She's immortal."

"Nothing's immortal. I just have to think outside the box."

"What if they get you again? Next time they won't settle for just torture and captivity."

"That's not happening. I won't let it. They only got the jump on me last time because they looked like you and Raph. I'm not going to let my guard down like that ever again."

"It's almost like we need a password. . ."

"Yeah. . ."

"How is she even an Elite? She's a girl."

"She was a maid that worked at the Estate. When you slit Mills' throat, she was the person who got him out of there and kept him alive long enough for a Reaper to come in and inject him with Rebirth. I guess he was grateful because he decided to have her put in a competition where she could face four other candidates to be his new Eve. She won. After that, she was put in Matthew's old role."

"How do you know all this?"

"She bragged about it every day."

The icicles drip against the momentary hush.

The sky is orange.

"I can't lose you, again." I choke back the heaving emotion.

"And you won't. You got your revenge, and now I have to get mine."

"She'll be taken care of when the riots start."

"I want to be the one who does it."

"But—"

"Please?"

"Please what?"

"Please support me. I can't do this without you."

I don't want to say yes. I want her to leave everything behind and go with me.

I'm such a hypocrite.

"Aren't you scared?" I ask. "Scared of dying, or being tortured again?"

"No, not really."

"Why? How?"

"Because I have you, and I know you won't let anyone hurt me."

"Are you kidding? You were just held captive for over a month. I didn't prevent anything."

"I think the whole experience has made you a bit more protective." Despite the blood running from her eyes she manages a wink. "I feel pretty safe around you."

I pull her in closer. "I love you."

Her breath warms my chest. "I love you too."

A tall, wide electronic billboard flickers in the distance. What once was an ad for some furniture store is now a live video feed. A decorated armchair waits in the middle of a bright room filled with bookcases, and a diamond chandelier hangs from the ceiling.

Mills steps into the feed, taking a seat in the chair. His cane rests on his lap.

His face is pale and cold. His eyes narrow, and his jaw tenses.

"Hello, my dear citizens." Each word he speaks leaks the rage within. "Dusk is approaching, and after the horrid events that took place this morning at the Boston, Massachusetts State House, I have decided to lift tonight's curfew nationwide."

Chloe shifts in my arms. "What?"

Mills' grips his cane without ease. "These are the photos of the remaining members of Lazarus. If you are hearing this through your stereo, look to the nearest billboard or television to see their faces." The screen flashes pictures of Chloe, Raphael, Exodus, Dante, and me. "These five terrorists are tearing away at our great country. They revolted against us all, wanting to secure my power for themselves." The pictures of us remain. "I am offering everlasting amnesty to anyone who kills even just *one* out of these five extremists. Laws will no longer apply to you, and I will personally finance your every need for the rest of your life. No more slaving away at your nine to five, no more paying your monthly tax to me, and no more worrying about your future. You will be praised at my side, living in glory, wealth, and fame."

A female inaudibly speaks off camera.

He hushes her.

"Curfew will not resume until they are found and killed. None of you are required to show up to your jobs until they are deceased and firing employees while we are pursuing these parasites is forbidden. Each city will have a drop off location guarded by Reapers. To confirm a kill, remove the head from the radical and bring it to one of these stations. There, a Reaper will examine it, and if deemed authentic, you will be brought to me, and your permanent amnesty shall be granted." Mills clears his throat. "These pictures will remain on every screen until the threat has been taken care of. Happy hunting, my dear citizens."

Mills' voice is cut off, but the images remain.

My mind can't find a response.

The city sounds are completely silenced. I can't hear the traffic anymore.

The door to our motel room swings open. Exodus signals us to him, "Get in here, now."

Chloe and I hurry inside, and he shuts the door.

Raphael stares at the tv. His face is riddled with disbelief. "No way. . ."

Dante throws his artificial fist, crashing it through the drywall, "There's not a chance in hell we make it past this, Ramirez."

"Shut up! Let me think."

"We can't leave," Chloe says, wiping her crimson tears from earlier. "We have to stay here."

Exodus grits his teeth. "Someone's bound to find us."

"Like who?" she asks.

There's a violent thud at the door.

Raphael swears, rushing toward the disturbance. Another thud breaks the lock, and the door flies open.

The hotel clerk wears a plaid button-up shirt with a baseball bat in his hands. "I knew I recognized those pictures from somewhere."

Before he can step further, a bullet rips through his head. Dante steps closer, firing two more rounds into his body as he collapses to the floor.

He turns to us, his black hair and trimmed beard distorted from the sunset shining through the open door, "I know where we can go."

CHAPTER NINE

The five of us blend in with the crazed crowds. Our faces are disguised by t-shirts wrapped around our mouths. The city plunges further into chaos by the minute.

My thoughts are on autopilot as we reach the edge of town. Survival is the only thing on my mind.

We reach an old gas station where Dante hotwires some poor bastard's car, to which we all get in and drive away without any hesitation.

The Saints don't stop us as we pass checkpoint after checkpoint due the large masses wildly searching for the faces that Mills plastered on every screen available. The booming city that once surrounded us turns into forest covered countryside. A road sign informs us that Cheshire is only a dozen miles away.

"So, where's this place you're taking us?" I ask from the backseat. Chloe and Exodus sit quietly next to me.

Dante glances at the rearview mirror. "There's an old train that sits on some abandoned tracks. It's been there for a decade or two. Since it's out of sight, Mills never cared to get rid of it. It's in the forest surrounding Cheshire. You ever been?"

"The first time I left Boston was after I was killed, so no," I mutter.

"It's gorgeous. I took Julie there all the time when she was a little girl."

The mention of his daughter gets my brain rolling, but I shut the memories down immediately. I'm so sick of thinking. I'm sick of the past. Why won't my mind ever just shut the *hell* up? Can't I ever just have a single moment of content? I'm being hunted—the last thing I need is to feel guilt, or sorrow.

I'd do anything to forget.

I don't want to remember Julie, Simon, my parents, Tommy, Marcy, *anyone*.

Raphael, who's riding shotgun, glances back at me, a handgun on his lap, "The only thing we can do now is hide away until Cass sends the footage."

"How will we know when she does?" I ask.

Dante chimes in, "I'll head into Cheshire every couple of days and use one of the computers at the library. She has a detailed list of instructions on how to send it to me without the data being tracked."

"Smart."

"I know."

Chloe's gentle snore directs my attention to her face resting on my shoulder. Exodus is looking out the window, carefully rubbing his covered forearm.

"You good?" I ask.

"Yeah, I just. . . the scenery is so eerie. It feels like a bunch of ax murderers are going to jump out of the trees and chop us up into little pieces."

"Just wait until it's day." Dante's focused on the road. "It's much prettier, then."

We drive in silence for a while, and I start to doze off.

Despite hating the past, it's all I dream about. The second I realize I'm reliving a memory, dream-me takes a pistol and puts it in his mouth.

At least that's new. . .

What's wrong with me?

"This is our stop." Dante's voice startles me awake. "We have to walk the rest of the way."

"But it's freezing out," Exodus complains. "Look, it's freaking snowing."

Chloe lifts her head off my shoulder. "Wait, we're here already?"

Raphael unbuckles himself, "Yeah, come on."

"Can't we just sleep in the car?" Exodus asks. "There's heat in here at least."

"Get out, Blaine," Dante orders.

"Ugh, fine."

He throws his hood up, opening the door.

Chloe and I follow.

Snow is falling from the blackened sky. The tall trees that surround us project dancing shadows.

Dante pulls out a flashlight, illuminating a wooden gate ahead of us. A sign planted next to it warns that beyond this point was unregulated, dangerous, and private property belonging to the government.

It's quiet a moment before Exodus mutters, "So friendly looking. Huh, Dante?"

Dante steps toward the gate. "Are you on your period, kid? Need a pad?"

"Maybe I do. I've got a heavy flow."

Chloe groans, "Groooosss."

I suppress my laugh, "Kinda funny."

"Focus," Raphael says, hopping over the gate.

We follow his lead. Once we're on the other side, Dante scrutinizes the scenery ahead.

"It should be about a mile straight ahead," he says, picking up his pace as he treads through the snow. "Come on, if we hurry, we can be there in about fifteen minutes."

"Fifteen minutes in the snow?" Chloe asks, heading off after him. "What is this? Highschool cross country?"

I sigh, forcing my feet to move.

THE TRAIN IS LONG BUT BROKEN APART FROM YEARS OF exposure. The woodland around is overgrown, giving the environment a surreal vibe.

"How do you propose we don't freeze to death tonight?" I ask as we climb into one of the train's larger compartments.

Raphael pulls out a box of matches. "You know I never leave home without these."

Exodus is shivering. "Great, now we just need some twigs and other fire-starting crap."

"Who's gonna go get it?" Chloe's shivering as well.

"It's going to be hard with everything being frozen and wet." Dante heads back outside. "Here, I'll go get us some firewood. Just hang tight and try to reduce your risk of hypothermia by moving around. Two of you should explore the rest of the train, while the other two stay here and make room for a fire and a place for us all to sleep."

"Jason and I can explore the train," Chloe volunteers.

Raph gives us a thumbs up. "I guess that means Blaine and I will stay here and make this place our temporary home."

Dante disappears after tossing me an extra flashlight. Chloe and I make our way down the large compartment to a door.

Glancing behind my shoulder, I say, "Have fun."

"You too," Exodus shoots back.

The next two compartments we check are ravaged with trash, graffiti, and rotten food. Each one matches the size and length of the one we're staying in, but they were each used for a different purpose. The entire time we explore, Chloe tries to joke around with me, bringing up the most bizarre topics to make me laugh. I humor her, of course, but my heart still aches that she won't just run away and leave with me.

"Come on, I think this is the last one," she says as we approach another door.

I'm losing all feeling in my fingers. "I hope so."

She opens the door, and I flash my beam into the cab. Past all the switches, levers, and buttons, the area is empty.

She looks at me. "Hey."

"Hey, what?"

"I know you're upset that we aren't leaving."

"What makes you say that?"

She shoots me an unimpressed look. "You aren't good at hiding your emotions."

Her words offend me. "Well, what do you want me to do? Bitch and moan until you change your mind?"

"Why can't you see where I'm coming from?"

"I do."

"Okay, then tell me. Tell me where I'm coming from."

"You want Robyn dead. You won't be able to be at peace until she is. So, yeah, I get it. I felt the same way with Matthew."

"Then why are you still upset?"

"Because I don't want anything else to happen to you, Chloe. I spent months trying to find you. I thought you were done for, and now that I finally have you back, you just want to go and put yourself back in danger."

"What about Raphael? You're his heir."

"He made me his heir. I didn't ask for it."

"He's one of our best friends. And what about Exodus? Dante? We can't just leave them behind and make them do this by themselves."

"I'm selfish, okay? I know I am, but the thought of you dying—"

"Neither of us are going to die."

"You can't say that. We don't have any more Rebirth, so if we're killed, it's over."

"We can steal some from an outpost."

"Are you kidding? Every person in this nation is hunting us, right now. If we're so much as seen..."

"We'll find a way."

"We can't keep cheating death. We should be dead—all of us—but we keep bending death over and screwing him. I'm worried our luck is running out. Dante has a plan that barely includes us. We're just waiting for Cass to send over the footage, and then boom, the population rises and overthrows the government. We can leave."

Her green eyes are mesmerizing. "The second this is over, I promise I'll leave with you. We can go and be together wherever you want, just please stay and help me—help us."

There's a sour taste in my mouth, but she wants closure, and if that means just a few more months of hell, then okay.

"For you, I will."

She gives me a hug, pressing her lips against mine. It's addicting.

Suddenly the butterflies in my stomach are replaced with dread.

Staying here, with Lazarus, is going to be the death of me.

CHAPTER TEN

A few days pass uneventfully. In the mornings, Chloe and I search for firewood while Raphael and Exodus hang back in the train. Since he's mastered a few tricks, Exodus keeps himself entertained. Raphael found an old can of spray paint, so to keep himself busy, he tags the train with cool artwork. Dante went into town yesterday morning. It's dusk now, and none of us have heard from him.

"It's almost been two days," Exodus says. The fire inside the compartment is dimming out. "Should we go find him?"

Raphael gazes into the embers. "He took the car, and I have no idea how to get into town."

"Me neither," I add.

Chloe's stomach growls, "I'm getting really hungry."

Exodus rubs his forearm, grimacing. "Yeah, me too."

I notice the fabric near his wrist is red. "You're bleeding."

He glances up. "It's nothing. . . I got a little injured back at the State House, but with everything going on, I haven't had the chance to patch it up."

This catch's Raphael's attention. "Is it infected? It's taking a long time to heal."

"I don't know."

"Lift up your sleeve."

He does as he's told, and all of us cringe at the sight. There's a stab wound below his wrist; the flesh is still split apart. Yellowish-pink ooze protrudes from it.

"Why didn't you tell us you were stabbed?" Raphael asks. Concern walks across his face. "We don't have any medical supplies."

He keeps his sleeve rolled up. "There's been a lot going on. I didn't think it was that important."

"Of course, it's important, don't be stupid. What exactly happened?"

"That Reaper stabbed me with some weird looking knife."

I get to my feet. "You should've said something. Here, I'll look for something to wrap it up."

Chloe scoots over, grabbing his wrist. More pus oozes out as she examines it. "This is really bad." She turns to Raphael. "We have to get him into town to see a doctor."

"And get our heads sawed off? What type of plan is that?" Raphael stands, looking my way. "You find anything, Jay?"

"No," I reply. "We've used all the cloth left in here."

"What about the other parts of the train?"

"Chloe and I already grabbed everything."

"You sure?"

"Positive."

He swears.

The already partially opened door to the compartment swings wide, surprising us.

It's just Dante, carrying a bunch of bags.

My lungs deflate, "You scared the piss out of me,"

He steps in further. "Good. You should never feel at ease. It'll get you killed."

Raphael sighs, "You're really good at disappearing without any trace, you know that? We've been waiting over twenty-four hours for you to check a computer."

Dante sets the bags down on a makeshift table. "*And* get us food, *and* get us medical supplies—"

"Medical supplies?" Chloe interrupts, getting to her feet. "Phew. Okay, good. Exodus was stabbed back at the State House and never told us."

Dante looks over. "Why didn't you say anything?"

"Oh," Exodus says. "I don't know. Maybe because everyone and their dog is trying to kill us, and I didn't want to be a burden?"

Dante reaches into one of the bags, grabbing some gauze and rubbing alcohol. "Is it infected?"

Exodus flashes his wound.

Dante's eyes widen. "That's not good at all, kid."

"You're telling me."

"Here, let me fix you up."

A loud rhythmic chime loudly echoes across the compartment. We all flinch. A sudden bright blue light flashes from Exodus's opened wound.

Dante freezes, "Oh no. No, no, *no, no*—!" He reaches for his gun, but a bullet blasts his face apart, painting the wall behind him red.

"*No!*" Raphael screams.

My mind shatters as Exodus points the smoking barrel of a pistol at me. I drop to the floor before he shoots. Raphael lunges at him, wrestling him into submission.

Exodus is somehow stronger. He flips Raphael to his side before straddling him, gun still in hand.

I jump to my feet. "*Blaine!*" I wrap my fingers around his throat. "*What are you doing!*"

He chokes, still fighting Raphael for the gun.

Another shot is fired. A bullet rips through the ceiling.

I reel my body back, taking him to the floor with me.

My vision blackens as he elbows me in the nose.

I sputter.

Another elbow.

Something breaks in my face.

I refuse to let go of his throat.

Chloe rushes in. She kicks Exodus in the face.

He doesn't stop fighting.

"Get the gun out of his hand!" I bellow, taking a third elbow.

She grabs the gun.

Exodus won't let go.

The trigger is pulled again.

The bullet misses her and nearly hits Raphael in the face.

A primal scream emerges from my throat. I choke him harder.

He elbows me again, and again, and again.

My vision grows dark.

I taste blood. It's coming from my mouth and nose. My face is raw.

Raphael scrambles to his feet, grabbing a pipe laying on the ground.

My body tenses. He slams the weapon down on the bridge of Exodus's nose, splitting it.

He stops struggling and goes limp.

I let go, rolling him off me. The excess amount of blood in my mouth spews all over as I hack and cough.

Pain. So much pain.

The beeping and flashing from Exodus's wound stops. The train drowns in silence.

My thoughts run rampant.

What the hell just happened? Were we just betrayed?

Raphael scrambles to Dante's side. To my utter surprise, he's still breathing. It's shallow, and faint, but there's still life in him.

I sit up, my head spinning. "He's alive?"

Dante coughs. Blood spews into the air.

I crawl toward him. The bullet turned his jaw into slush. Crimson is pooling out like a waterfall.

Raphael grits his teeth, "You're going to be okay."

Dante tries to speak, "M-mind c-c-control."

I turn away. It's too much.

He struggles to breathe, spitting instead. The back of my neck is splashed with his fluids. After a few seconds, he's gone, and the train is silent once more.

Dante. The last person from my life before death. Dead.

Mind control? Was it Rewired? No, it couldn't be, there were no numbers, no orders given.

Chloe kneels next to me. She checks out my crooked nose. "Are you okay?"

Red tears spill down my cheeks, mixing in with the rest of the bloody mess, "Why can't we catch a break?"

Raphael stumbles over to Exodus's motionless body, getting to the ground and staring at his wrist, "Mind control. Through a stab wound? Wait. I think I remember Vice telling me about this."

Chloe fails to hide her distress. "About what?"

"But it was only a protype a little while ago. How—?"

"Are you going to tell us what you're talking about?" flames pulse through my face. "Or are you going to continue monologuing?"

"A knife. I forget what it's called, but when you stab someone with it, there's a button on the handle, that when pressed, will inject a tiny chip into the bloodstream. This chip will corrupt its victims with an urge to kill, and when activated, sends them into a murdering spree. Kinda like Rewired."

"So, he wasn't in control?" Chloe asks.

Raphael shakes his head, "No, and he won't remember anything once he snaps out of it. Which, judging by the absence of the blue light and ringing coming from his wrist, I'd say has already happened."

"Will it trigger again?" I spit out some blood.

"It does it randomly. Nobody's controlling it, but that's bad, because that means it could be activated at any given moment throughout any given day."

"Can we take the chip out?"

"Yeah, maybe if we had a small EMP blast, or that serum Dante used to deactivate the bombs inside our heads, but with everyone trying to kill us it's going to be tough to find."

"So, what do we do? We can't take it out."

Chloe thinks for a moment. "Could we tie him up until we get something to destroy the chip?"

"He'd freeze to death," Raphael mutters. Blood wells up in his one visible eye. "Damn it. . . we're going to have to—"

"Have to what?" I interrupt.

"Kill him."

CHAPTER ELEVEN

I drive down the quiet, dark, and snowy road with trees swaying gently on either side. When Dante came back, he didn't bring the original car he stole. He found a gray sedan that came with a working key.

Exodus is still unconscious, buckled in the seat next to me. Raphael sits directly behind him in the back.

I have the radio turned on. The music isn't loud.

I wish I didn't see Dante like that. I wish I didn't see the lower half of his face blown apart. My heart pounds, picking up speed at the thought of what Raph and I have to do next.

It isn't fair. Nothing is.

He had no control over what he was doing. His mind was altered.

Nothing is going according to plan. There's only a few of us left, and I have no idea how we're going to receive anything from Cass now that Dante's dead.

Hopeless. Rock bottom. Tears trace down my flushed face.

I can't handle much more of this.

Some time passes. As I'm taking a left down another back road, Exodus opens his eyes.

"Wait. . ." He blinks. "Where are we?"

Cat's got my tongue.

"We're taking you into town to fix your arm," Raphael lies. He isn't skilled at hiding the pain in his voice.

"How long was I out?"

"A while."

"Where's everyone else?"

My mind reviews tonight's carnage as it displays across the night's snowy scenery. I clear my throat, "They're back at the train. Dante's making dinner."

"That sounds nice." He stops, grimacing as he touches his face. "Woah, why am I bleeding? My face hurts like hell." He finally notices me. "And what happened to you? There's blood everywhere, man."

Raphael chimes in, "You passed out from all the pain in your arm, and while Jason was taking you to the car, he tripped, and the both of you went face-first into a tree."

"Oh." He stares down at his feet. I can tell he doesn't believe us. "Well, how long until we're in town?"

"I don't know. Maybe fifteen minutes?" I say. My throat threatens to close.

"Are you okay, man?"

"Yeah, I'm just having a hard time."

"Something happened, didn't it. . .?"

"What do you mean?"

"You guys are acting really off, and I can't remember anything."

"Because you passed out. Look, I'm just nervous because people might recognize us."

"You would never leave Chloe alone after what she was just through. Not unless you absolutely had to."

"She's not alone. She has Dante."

"Where's my gun?"

I'm unable to answer.

Exodus lets out a small sigh. The car goes quiet as I take another left.

I glance at him. "Exodus—"

"Stop calling me that."

"That's what we've always called you."

"That was a nickname I was given in Salem. I'm not in Salem anymore."

"Okay, I'm sorry."

More silence. He reaches for the radio, switching the station and turning it up, dissipating some of the tension with the sound of melodic jazz.

From the rearview mirror, Raphael grabs his gun with blood streaming from his eyes. He lifts it, pointing the barrel at the back of Blaine's head.

The music picks up. I grit my teeth.

Blaine lets out a pained smile, eyes turning red. "At least it's a pretty night. . ."

Blood drips from my nose as we hit a bump. Tears waterfall down my face. I can't keep calm.

Through the rearview mirror, Raphael wraps his finger around the trigger, his bottom lip quivering.

My legs tremble.

Raphael wraps his finger around the trigger.

Blaine sniffles, his bottom lip trembling.

"You were supposed to play dumb, you idiot!" Raphael cries, the gun shaking in his grip. "Why did you catch on! I hate you!"

Blaine shudders, tears splashing against his lap. "I'm sorry, man."

"Why did you have to come into my life and make me care about you! You became family! You remind me so much of my little brother! I'm such a dumbass!" Raphael drops the gun, slamming his fist against a seat.

The music continues, the piano and guitar intertwining into a perfect melody.

I ease my foot down onto the brake, pulling off to the side of the snowy road, my vision blurred with blood.

Blaine's inconsolable, "What happened to me back there?"

I slide the back of my hand across my eyes. "When you were stabbed, a chip was planted inside your arm. It went off when Dante got back, and you killed him. . . The only way to stop it from happening again, is to use an EMP, but with everyone hunting us, there's no way we could get our hands on one."

"And you were going to put me down, so I didn't hurt anyone else."

"Yeah."

"I can't," Raphael's voice cracks. "I can't do it."

I stare at the steering wheel, shuttering out a sigh, "Neither can I."

Blaine buries his face in his palms. "I don't want to die."

Raphael unbuckles himself, opening the back door, "Switch me seats, Jay."

I nod, mimicking his actions. He gets behind the wheel.

"What are you doing?" Blaine asks.

Raphael flips a U-turn, heading back the way we came. "We're getting Chloe, then driving into town."

"That's a death sentence," I mumble.

"We're going to find a Saint, rough him up, then force him to drive us to the nearest outpost. They'll have EMPs there. They always do."

"Raph, that's suicide. All we have are pistols."

He ignores me, and we listen to the music still flowing through the speakers.

CHAPTER TWELVE

Cheshire is small bedroom community. Houses are spaced out, trees are planted everywhere, and people walk through the streets with their pets like nothing's wrong in the world.

It's weird seeing others out this late. Just a couple of days ago, if you were found out past curfew, you'd either be shot or abducted without reason.

Chloe and I sit in the back of the sedan. She didn't like the idea of infiltrating some outpost, but it sounded better than the alternative route we were supposed to take.

My sanity claws up the sides of my skull, desperately trying to stay intact. Dante's dead. I don't know how much more I can take. It's too much. All of this is too much.

I hate death. I know he's gone, but I keep trying to convince myself that he's waiting for us back at the train, maintaining the fire, or cooking dinner. All that's there is a disfigured corpse.

I'm in Hell, and there's no escape.

It burns.

Chloe rubs her thumb over my knee. I pull myself out of my head.

We already passed a checkpoint entering town, but there

weren't any Saints manning the station. Raphael keeps a sharp eye out for anyone in uniform.

"We've been looking for over an hour." Blaine's voice is laced with pessimism. "There's no use, man."

Raphael shakes his head. "You aren't going to convince me to stop."

Chloe lifts her head from my shoulder. "We could try the diner we passed a little bit ago?"

"Why would a Saint be at a diner?"

"I don't know, but all we're doing is driving up and down the same streets. We've passed the same couple walking their chihuahua three times already."

"Fine. I could use a coffee anyway." Raphael turns the car around, heading for Cheshire's business strip.

"Why are you guys wasting so much time on me?" Blaine tucks his chin. "I'm a killer. I killed Dante. I shouldn't be here. I'm just slowing you three down."

"Shut up," Raph mutters, glaring ahead. "We're saving you. End of discussion."

We pass the cemetery that's situated on both sides of the road. I stare out the window and see all the tombstones littering the gated grassy field to my left.

Death.

Dying.

Rotting.

Suffering.

Alone.

All alone.

Shut up. Stop thinking.

"You're being quiet," Chloe whispers. Her breath is warm against my ear.

I sigh, "I'm fine, just tired."

"We can get you a coffee at the diner. We have a long night ahead of us."

"I hate coffee, it tastes like dirt."

"Nu-uh."

"Uh-huh."

"Well, fine, we can get you an energy drink at a gas station, or something."

"That's a bit better."

She chuckles.

Raphael slams on the brakes, causing the car to lurch forward.

"Got one in sight." He points to an intersection. "He's smoking a cigarette next to his car."

I see the solider. From the looks of it, he's all alone.

"Okay so what's the plan?" Chloe asks.

"Just follow my lead. When I jump him, get in the back of his car. This bastard's going to take us to a base whether he likes it, or not," Raphael replies.

We pull up about twenty feet away. Raphael parks on the shoulder, and he steps out of the car.

We follow.

The Saint's back is to us. The intersection is dark and quiet. The only sounds come from the swaying trees as a light snow falls from the sky.

We're ten feet away when Raphael rushes the solider. Before the Saint can turn around, he's thrown to the ground.

"What the hell—"

Raphael stomps the back of his leg.

The solider bellows, getting lifted to his feet.

Chloe, Blaine, and I head for the patrol car.

Raphael gnashes his teeth. "You're going to drive us to the nearest outpost, got it?"

The Saint goes for his gun.

Raphael headbutts him, bashing his face down against the hood of the car, "I'll break your leg 'til your bones poke through your skin, *Gilipollas!*"

I open the back door. The three of us hop in. First Blaine, then Chloe, then me.

"You're going to take us, got it!" Raphael smashes the Saint's head against the hood once more.

"Okay, okay! I'll take you."

"No games, no nothing. If you call for backup, or pull any other dirty tricks, I'll kill you. You got a family?"

"Screw you."

Another slam into the hood. "I asked you a question!"

"I'm taking you where you want! There's no reason to torture me, you *parasite*!"

Raphael digs his hand into the man's back pocket, prying out his wallet. Using his left hand to hold him down, he uses his right to go through it.

"A wife and a little girl," he says, tugging a picture out.

"I'll kill you," the Saint whispers defiantly.

"Have fun with that." He guides the solider to the driver's side door. "Get in. I've got three people in the back who will light you up if you try anything."

The Saint complies.

TOWERING BUILDINGS SURROUND ME ON EVERY SIDE. The streets are filled with cars, and civilians are walking in and out of every store seeable. The sky is gloomy, and the moon is obscured. Our source of light comes from within the city we're swallowed by.

Albany, New York.

We've been driving for about an hour in complete silence. The tension in the air could be cut with a knife. The anxiety consuming me begs for an outburst.

We aren't ready to storm an outpost, kill every soldier in our way, and escape with an EMP grenade—especially not with a bunch of handguns as our only means of assault.

I know why Raphael's planning this, but acting reckless and getting us killed isn't the answer. Blaine's family, and I know he's an asset, not to mention my best friend. But Raph needs to take a step back and think. None of us will make it through tonight if we go in guns blazing. We need to find another way to get that chip out of Blaine's arm that won't get us ripped to shreds.

The patrol car comes to a stop at a red light. Thick traffic slows our commute.

The Saint speaks his first words since entering the car. "You aren't going to like where I'm taking you."

Raphael glares, "Why's that?"

"It's one of the most guarded outposts in the nation."

You're kidding.

Blaine takes his gun and shoves it into the back of the man's head, "Why the hell didn't you tell us that beforehand?"

The Saint grits his teeth, "Get that away from me."

Raphael cracks his neck with a head twist, then says, "So you're telling us that we're as good as dead if we step foot in the place? That all of this is for nothing?"

"Unless you're feeling suicidal, yeah, you're outta luck."

Raphael slams his knuckles into the dashboard. *"Damn it!* Listen here and listen good. Where can we get an EMP without getting holes ripped through our bodies?"

"Nowhere."

"Do you want me to kill you?"

"Oh, there really isn't a point for you to do that, anymore."

"And what makes you say that, smartass?"

He grins, "Look around. There are soldiers everywhere who're in position to slaughter you freaks the first chance they get. You do know that there's trackers in each of our cars topped with hidden mics and cameras, right? Being a part of Lazarus, I figured you would've known that. . . or have you just gotten sloppy?"

My gaze rapidly sweeps side to side. My heart sinks into the deepest pit. Around the corner to my right, two Reapers load magazines into their weapons. On the left, five Saints stare us down.

Raphael tilts his gun to the man's head, "I told you I was going to end you if you pulled this!"

"Oh, just you wait until *she* comes."

I panic as Raphael pulls the trigger. "Wait, they'll start shooting—!"

My ears burst, my vision flashing as a bullet flies from his barrel and through the Saint's face.

Blood spatters against the window.

Gunshots ring out. A collage of bullets slam against the car's exterior.

They don't pierce, but the windows spiderweb.

Blaine grabs the dead Saint by the arm, and with the help of me and Chloe, we drag him into the backseat and onto the floor.

Raphael gets behind the wheel. "We're gonna get out of this." He smears the gore from the window. "Just get ready to get out and open the trunk when I say so."

He speeds forward, bashing into the car in front of us. The driver swerves out of the way.

More bullets crash against the vehicle as Raphael takes a hard left, turning down another busy street.

The glass on either side of me is cracked. I look dead ahead, grabbing my gun from its holster.

I flip off the safety.

"Why did you shoot him?" Chloe asks.

The window to our left is about to give out.

"They were going to start shooting anyway!" Raphael retorts.

Three more Saints appear down the road. They fire multiple rounds into the windshield. The damage leaves us blind to the outside world.

Blaine grits his teeth, "Maybe not your best idea, Raph—"

The driver's side window gets pulverized. Glass shards shower us.

Raphael slams down on the horn, picking up speed.

I flash back just seconds before I was put into a coma all those months ago. The bitter sting of anxiety swims through my veins.

"You're going to hit something!" I shout. A bullet enters the car and destroys the stereo.

I'm vulnerable.

Die.

You're gonna die.

Not gonna make it.

Over.

Something collides with the hood of our car. A mangled Saint goes flying past the broken window.

Still zooming forward, Raphael grabs his gun from the passenger seat and fires multiple rounds into the windshield. It shatters, and up ahead, the light at the intersection turns red.

Due to the firefight, the cars ahead of us don't stop. Multiple collisions break out on all sides.

Raphael slams on the brakes. The snow beneath us makes the car skid. We crash into the already wrecked vehicles at a dangerous speed.

My seatbelt restrains me. My body lifts in the air, same with Chloe and Blaine, but Raphael flies through the windshield, bashing into the car ahead of us before smacking down on our hood.

I jerk forward as another vehicle hits us from behind.

Snow and glass fall in unison.

A swear springs from my lips. I try clicking the button that releases my buckle. It's jammed.

"Are you okay?" Chloe asks. Her eyebrow is split open. blood pours down her face.

I reach for my knife. It's sheathed through my belt loop. "Yeah, hold on."

I slash the belt, then hastily free both Chloe and Blaine.

The gunshots stop.

"Raphael," Chloe shouts. "You alive?"

He doesn't move, but I think I see him breathing through all the chaos around us.

People are sprinting from their vehicles, not caring that they're ruined. Everyone runs in different directions.

It psyches me out.

Where are the soldiers? Why did they stop shooting?

I shimmy my way through the broken window. Hitting the ground hard, I stumble to my feet, grateful that I'm still functioning and able to move.

I look at the pileup, but beyond that, Reapers and Saints visibly charge us from about a hundred yards away.

There's a woman in the car that crashed into us. She's unconscious, but I throw the thought of helping her from my mind as I approach the trunk of the patrol car. The other vehicle is crushed up against it, but I'm able to jimmy it open with my knife. A small arsenal appears, something I wasn't expecting.

"Chloe, Blaine!" I yell over the disorder. "Hurry, come here!"

The two of them exit the car, the snowfall growing thicker and faster. It masks us from unwanted eyes.

They approach the back of the trunk. We each grab a weapon.

"There's a bullet-proof vest," Blaine says, pointing to the far left of the compartment.

"Give it to Chloe," I yell, and he does.

She puts it on.

I hurry over to the front of the car, slipping in the process. Raphael's still on the hood, I turn his motionless body over.

Nothing looks broken, and there's only a bit of blood coming from his hands.

I tap him on the cheek, but nothing.

"Wake up!" I yell.

Still nothing.

A woman ahead of us collapses out of her car, her legs twisted.

"Raph!" I slap him as hard as I can. His eyes flash open.

He wakes with a start, "Jason?" his pupils are massive. He's concussed.

"You gotta get up, man. They're almost here."

He nods. I help him off the hood.

"Here." Chloe appears at our side and tosses Raphael a shotgun. "Take this."

Before he can thank her, we hear a voice in the distance blurt, "There! They're bundled up at the intersection."

My muscles tighten. "Get behind a car!"

A storm of bullets hurl our way as I dive over the hood of the patrol car. Chloe follows, but Raphael and Blaine sprint behind a crashed taxi.

I use both hands to grip my rifle, my knife still gripped in my left. "How do we get out of this?"

Chloe flinches as a random bullet flies overhead. "I don't know, but I'm pretty sure they only have a rough idea of where we are, and so with the snow and the wind, I bet we could stealth around and pick them off one by one."

My head tilts forward. The gunfire stops.

"Spread out!" the modulated voice of a Reaper orders. It sounds faint through the storm. "Find them!"

I put the rifle down in the snow. I then pat my holster, assuring my handgun is still secured. "Split up."

She quietly acknowledges me.

Both of us creep to opposite sides of the patrol car before disappearing into the cover of night.

Bright beams penetrate the snowy night. The lampposts that trail down both sides of the street also help illuminate some small areas, but the storm is obscuring almost everything.

A couple yards away, I make out the shape of a Saint. He doesn't have a flashlight, and his forearm is shielding his eyes from the icy wind.

I creep toward him. My knife is held tightly.

"Stop hiding!" he yells, but the only reply is a howling breeze.

I thrust my blade into the side of his throat, and then shove it into his temple.

He gags. I toss him to the street before creeping further.

Next to one of the cars, there's an abrupt gunshot, but the night quickly grows quiet again.

We'll make it out of this if the storm keeps going.

Please keep going.

I'm calm. I'm in control.

Another figure emerges ahead. It's another Saint.

Sneaking toward him, I stop when another appears by his side.

I think back to all my training. A wave of excitement surges through me.

One wrong move and I'm dead.

I creep closer.

"It's freezing out here," one of them mutters, his voice hardly audible.

"Hush. We don't want them to know where we are."

"Yeah, sorry."

I wrap my left hand around his neck and slash his throat, diving at his partner and piercing his jugular.

He instinctively fires his rifle multiple times into the air as the two of us barrel into the snow.

I rip the blade out and finish the job.

"Over here!" a modulated voice exclaims.

I hear the footfalls. Scrambling to my feet, I dive behind the nearest car and slide beneath it.

Two Reapers and a Saint step into view, hovering over their dead comrades.

You're all next.

The Saint glances back and forth between his two superiors. "They're sneaking through the snow and picking us off."

"So be it," one of them replies, a shotgun gripped in his hands. "It's only a matter of time before she shows up and kills them all."

The other Elite growls, "And I want to be far away from here when that happens."

They're talking about Robyn.

I slowly pull out my handgun.

"Can't we just leave?" the Saint asks.

One of them tries to reply, but I interrupt him with the squeeze of a trigger. A bullet blasts from my barrel and penetrates his mask. The other two aim toward me, but I blow several holes into their heads before they can do anything.

Chloe appears out of nowhere, blood sprinkled across her pretty face. "That was the last of them."

I slide out from beneath the car. My fingers are numb. "Are you sure?"

"Positive."

Raphael and Blaine appear through the snow.

"What now?" I ask. The snow falls even faster.

"We need to make it to that base," Raphael replies. Small pieces of glass stick out of his hands.

Blaine sighs, "No, that's too risky, and you're already hurt."

"So am I." Chloe glances down at her bleeding bicep.

"What happened?" I notice the wound.

"Just a graze," she says. "But it's bleeding really bad."

Raphael's visible eye narrows. "We didn't go through all of this just to give up now."

"This is my choice," Blaine interjects. "We're out of options, man. Sneaking into a military outpost, let alone the most guarded one in the nation, is suicide without better planning and more numbers."

"But you're a threat if we don't," Raphael says.

"Leave me here, then. I can switch up my look, get a new identity."

Chloe shakes her head. "Then what happens when the chip is triggered a second time, and you murder everyone around you?"

His face contorts. "I don't know, but I'm sure as hell not going to let the three of you die because of my cruddy luck. You guys gave me a second chance at life. I was going to rot in Salem forever, and you three changed my fate. I got to experience a lot more than I ever could've hoped for. Besides, getting married and having a kid, that's overrated anyway."

"I'm not giving up on you!" Spit flies from Raph's mouth. He throws his hands in the air. "We can't afford another loss."

Blaine argues some more. In the distance, helicopter blades rotate furiously against the air.

"Wait," I silence them all. "Do you guys hear that?"

They listen.

"A helicopter?" Chloe mutters.

It gets louder, and louder, and a bright spotlight beams down on us before we can run.

A military chopper hovers a hundred feet above. I only see the front of it due to the heavy snow, but I'm pretty sure there are miniguns attached to it.

A familiar woman's voice blares from the helicopter, *"Parasites!"*

Raphael flips the voice off.

Chloe's entire body trembles as she grits her teeth.

Robyn.

CHAPTER THIRTEEN

The helicopter descends, and the four of us raise our weapons. The miniguns mounted to the chopper rotate, so we hesitantly lower our guns.

Breathing becomes more difficult.

She can't die. How do we kill someone who can't die?

The helicopter now only hovers a little way from the street. A figure jumps from the exposed side, landing perfectly in the snow.

The chopper raises back into the air. Its spotlight shines on us like a second moon.

Robyn stares at the four of us, her contorted smile and her exaggerated features look more twisted in the storm. Her trench coat blows in the wind as she takes a step forward.

Chloe lifts her gun. "Whore! You dirty, rotten *slut!*"

"Are you still bitter?" Robyn glares with animalistic eyes. "Drop your weapons, or I'll have you all shredded to pieces. You know, I'd prefer that. I'll get a little taste of all your insides."

I glance up at the miniguns, then back down at her.

My hands twitch. Do I shoot her, or do I toss the gun and think of something else?

Raphael throws his gun to the street. "Fine."

We follow his lead. Chloe's the last to let go.

Robyn steps closer. "Raphael Ramirez, the Head of Lazarus."

Raphael grins wildly, his eyes wide with bloodlust. "The one and only."

"I like you. I like the ones who think they're king," Robyn says while licking her lips. She reaches into her coat. "Is your mama proud? Oh. That's right. . . she died on her birthday, along with your gangster father, and your little brother, Santiago."

Raphael suddenly reaches for his concealed knife. "Say his name again, and you die!"

"Highly unlikely." She laughs like a hyena. "Master was right, it's so fun seeing you mad!"

Her trench coat flaps against the wind, revealing a small, metal sphere dangling from her belt. My heart jumps into my throat.

No freaking way...

It's an EMP grenade.

I suppress a smile while devising a plan.

I decide to start taunting her. "You know he's going to kill you once you've outlived your purpose, right?" I step forward, leaving my arms at my side. "He doesn't care about you."

Her face twists. The over exaggeration of every single muscle startles me, "Don't play stupid games with me, Pinder." Saliva spits from her lips and her eyes expand even more. "I know everything about you. You may have briefly put my Brenix down, but that didn't stop us from learning every trick of yours while they were functional."

I move even closer, and she stands her ground. "You're just a breeder," I sneer, my lips tug into a little smile. "Once you give him children, he'll kill you like the rest."

"*Liar!*" she pulls a hidden knife out of nowhere and lunges at me.

I dodge, yanking the EMP grenade from her waist and clicking the button at the top.

"*Blaine!*" I yell. The device beeps in my hand.

He rushes toward me.

"*No!*" Robyn screams.

An electromagnetic pulse pushes into the air. It knocks me off my feet and into the snow, leaving my ears ringing.

The helicopter's engine screams while the blades malfunction.

Crap!

I scuttle backward in the snow as the chopper turns sideways. It glides into a large building across the street, tearing through the structure. The blades break and fly in several directions.

Robyn's on the ground. It looks like she's having a seizure.

I get to my feet, dazed and disorientated. Chloe, Raphael, and Blaine do the same.

I can barely hear anything over the ringing in my ears.

Robyn slowly stops seizing. A foreign emotion appears on her face.

Fear.

She's immortal. What does she have to be afraid of?

I stop. It all clicks. Dante's words from the rooftop echo through my skull.

"*The Maiden's Touch is a product of reverse engineered Rebirth with its effects amplified ten-fold.*"

Before her demise, Marcy told me how Rebirth works. Millions of tiny nanobots are injected into the body to repair the damage from the inside. They're fit with electricity to jump-start the heart in the event of a host's death.

Nanobots. . .

Electricity. . .

A wicked grin creeps across my face. "So, that's her weakness. An EMP."

Robyn struggles to sit up. "T—That's not true. *You know absolutely nothing!*"

Chloe practically foams at the mouth. "You're going to pay for what you did to me, you *whore.*"

Closing in, she kicks her old torturer in the face. Her head bounces off the snowy asphalt, black ooze exploding from her nostrils.

Chloe kicks a few more time, adding a nasty stomp.

Robyn cries out, abruptly grabbing the knife she dropped and hurling it into Chloe's thigh.

She stumbles back.

I rush in, stomping Robyn's leg.

She screams, reaching into her coat and flinging something at me.

A throwing knife plants deep in my shoulder.

"*You prick!*" I gnash my teeth.

She scrambles to her feet, pulling a pistol out and wildly aiming it between the four of us. "Stand down! I'll k-kill. . . I'll shoot! Get back!"

Raphael steps closer. So does Blaine.

Chloe keeps the knife in her thigh, grimacing. "You're going to rot in hell."

I scan the ground for our guns, but they were pushed back in the blast. The constant downfall of snow makes them impossible to find.

That doesn't matter.

We're going to slaughter her.

Moving closer, I say, "Where's that wide grin of yours?"

She snarls, black spilling from her eyes and mouth. "You've been a pain long enough!"

Turning to me, she fires. With a moving target, harsh wind, and low visibility, the bullet misses.

I bull rush her, tackling her to the ground and smacking the gun out of her hand.

She tries to gouge my eyes out.

I thrash my head to the side, chomping down on her middle finger.

A horrified shrill fills the air. I crunch down as hard as I can and black blood floods my mouth. Ripping the finger from her hand, I spit the gore across her ugly face.

Raphael kicks her in the side of the head. A brutal attack ensues from the four of us.

Stomping.

Kicking.

Punching.

Choking.

The snow beneath us turns black, and with each strike more adrenaline fuels me.

Her breathing grows shallow and wet.

I get off her.

Chloe finds Robyn's pistol on the street.

Despite the hundreds of crashed cars, the mangled helicopter, and the relentless storm, the chaos around us fades into nothingness.

A victory after so many losses.

Raphael wipes black from his cheek. "We did it. We know how to kill these freaks now."

I let out a pained smile. The throwing blade is still in my shoulder. "We also saved Blaine, and it's all because of your recklessness."

His black hair is messy, blowing around in the wind. "I had to do it. Who else would step in if we fought?" he chuckles. A rarity. "And hey, look on the bright side. None of us died."

"But if we continue to stay here, that'll change."

He turns to Chloe. "Frye?"

Her gun is aimed down at Robyn's head. "What?"

"Make sure she can't come back."

She nods, but there's a shift, and we all look over.

Robyn is now weakly propped up. She holds a black ballpoint pen, the tip pointed at Raphael. "Did you know that the name Raphael means *God has healed*?"

She clicks the pen and a blade springs from the tip. Chloe pulls the trigger again and again, ripping trails through her skull.

The city lies in silence. I turn.

There's no trace of my heart. I can't feel it. "Raph. . .?"

The blade is lodged deep inside Raphael's eye socket, blood oozing from his tear duct.

His mouth slowly opens. He loses his balance.

"What?" Blaine catches him. "Dude? *Dude?*"

"W-W-W-Where?" Raphael's body convulses.

More crimson spills from his eye. His tremors increase in intensity.

My legs refuse to support my weight.

My vocal cords freeze.

His words vibrate with his body. Excess spit slurs him, "Ja-Jason? Eveefing's *black!* Am-Am I *thying?*"

I blink. Blink some more.

Blink.

Blink.

Blink.

He howls, ripping at the blade.

Too abrupt. Too sudden. What the hell is going on? What just happened?

It's too hard to breathe. I start yelling, "K-knock it off. . . You're okay, man. It's barley in there."

Drool pools from his mouth. His tremors crescendo and then, they slow.

All life fades. His rattling stops.

I stare, shaking his shoulders. "Raph? Raph, stop screwing around. . ."

Nothing. No reply.

He's limp.

A corpse.

Both my tears and jaw drop in unison. I throw myself at his corpse, knocking Blaine back.

"Raphael?" the gun in Chloe's hand fumbles to the snow.

Blaine collapses, muffling out a sob.

I turn to Robyn's carcass. "What did you do! What the hell did you just do!"

I stumble to my feet, but before I'm able to cave her skull in with the sole of my shoe, sirens overpower the deafening wind.

"Jason." Chloe grabs my arm, pulling me out of my withering rage. "More are coming."

Red, white, and blue lights flash through the falling snow. "I'll kill them all!"

Her face is flushed. "No. I can't lose you, too. We've gotta go."

Our gaze meets. She's right.

Blaine scoops Raphael up in his arms, scrambling to his feet.

No words. Just silence. The three of us leave the carnage behind.

Another part of my soul is gone forever.

CHAPTER FOURTEEN

Trees dance in the dark and snow flurries through the air, covering three shattered beings. The street outside the cemetery is desolate, and the lights from the town are drowned out by the storm.

There's no feeling in my fingers as I push a shovel into the frozen dirt.

Different shades of blood stain my pale face.

Chloe puts a hand on my shoulder. Her voice is soft, "Maybe we should do this in the morning?"

I can't muster a shake of the head. "No. The town is asleep. Now's the best time."

She doesn't say anything. I scoop out another small pile of dirt, the hole growing deeper.

Blaine kneels next to Raphael. He's saying things I can't hear over the frigid wind.

That's probably a good thing.

Guilt. Nothing but guilt. I should've demanded we stay here. I should've restrained him when he grew reckless, and because I didn't, he's not breathing anymore.

I think back to a month ago. Him and I were inside that

cramped motel room, arguing before getting into a fight. I punched him in the face, told him to go to hell, and almost pulled a gun. Now he's dead.

I think he was right. . . I *am* the reason for all of this. I am the reason why everyone around me fades. I'm a bringer of death, and it's only a matter of time before Chloe and Blaine meet a violent end because of me.

I feel the weight of my gun. I want to bring it up to my head and rid this guilt from my chest. How easy would it be? I could just put a bullet in my brain, and all of this would be over.

I want to die.

I could end this now.

It would only take two seconds.

The fantasy vanishes at the thought of Chloe witnessing my brain escape the back of my skull. It would rock her to her core.

She doesn't need more trauma.

She needs to heal, not to break further.

Still. . . it sounds peaceful to be dead. A permanent sleep. No more violence, no more sadness, no more guilt. It would all be gone, and I would be resting.

Forever.

I keep digging, and a little while later, the grave is ready. I toss the shovel to the ground, and with Blaine's help, we lower Raphael into the ground.

Blaine says his goodbyes first. Afterward, he turns his back to us and walks away.

"Hey, where are you going?" Chloe asks.

He shrugs, "I don't know. . . I think I might go get plastered."

"Do you want to wait for us?"

"No, not really."

He disappears, and I gaze into the open grave, acutely aware of my own beating heart.

Raphael's mouth is still opened. The sight sends a shiver down my spine.

Chloe says her goodbyes. I follow. To be honest, I'm not even conscious of what I'm saying. I'm on auto pilot. The only thing that's clear is that I've said a lot. When I finally stop, Chloe picks up the shovel and fills the hole with dirt.

One last look at Raph. Then, he's gone, consumed by earth.

The snow starts to die down.

I sit next to the grave, lowering my face into my palms.

Chloe drops next to me. "What do we do now?"

It takes me a second to respond. "I don't really know anymore."

"Me neither."

"There's only three of us left, four if you include Cass."

"I know. . . That's not a lot."

"Chloe?"

"Yeah?"

"I don't want to be here anymore."

She delicately puts her head on my shoulder. "Don't say that."

"What's going to happen when you're next? Or Blaine? Or even me?"

"Well, I can tell you one thing."

"What?"

"We died fighting for what we believed in."

"My mind is fried. I don't know if we stay here or leave, or what we do."

"It's simple. We change up our looks. We blend in with the public and lay low for a bit."

"But what about the Maiden's Touch?"

"It's going to have to wait. Clearly, they're still testing it or else we'd all be dead by now, so let's not worry about it for a bit."

I take a deep breath, wiping the red from my eyes. "You're right. Dante said Cass had a way of communicating with him when she was ready. I think that means there might be some type of device on his body that he used. Let's go back to the train, search him, then bury him. If he has anything, we'll wait until she reaches out, then go along with our original plan."

"Just lead the way. I'll always follow you," Chloe whispers.

"I don't get why."

"You're worth it, and I trust you."

Her words should comfort me, but they don't. The thought of her dying has caused many restless nights, and with everything that has just happened, I know my insomnia has just begun. She won't be safe until this is over, and that kills me.

I'm nothing without her.

"Please. . .," I creak.

"Please?"

"Don't leave me."

"I won't. I promise."

She rests her head on my shoulder, and I cry.

I cry harder than ever before.

CHAPTER FIFTEEN

FIVE MONTHS LATER

Rain streams down the window as trees outside sway side to side. The sky is gray, and faint music plays overhead as the smell of pancakes linger in the air.

I stare out the window, trying my best to ignore the reflection that stares back.

I don't want to see my dyed, messy black hair.

I don't want to see my unshaven face or the black framed glasses.

I just want to watch the rain and forget I exist, which is too much to ask for when your brain is wired to run as fast as it possibly can. I'm always thinking, worrying, and killing my sanity with every passing moment.

I'm tired of thinking of the same things repeatedly.

There's only so much left that can crumble before I'm gone.

"Mr. Valentine?" A woman approaches me in the reflection.

I eye the plate of pancakes in her hands. "Oh, thank you."

She sits the plate down on the booth's table before placing syrup and butter next to it. "No, thank you."

I hand her five dollars. "You always make the best breakfast, Suzy."

"Well, you and your wife make the best regulars. Say, where is she this morning?"

"She decided to sleep in, but she'll be here tomorrow."

Suzy Chindin is the owner of the only diner in Cheshire. She and her four kids run the place. She reminds me so much of my own mom.

It's comforting.

"Well good," she smiles. "I love seeing her beautiful green eyes every morning."

"That makes two of us."

Her smile remains as she walks away. "Well, you enjoy your breakfast, Mr. Valentine." she takes a few steps, stops, then turns back. "Actually, I've been meaning to ask you something."

My throat tightens. "Oh? What's that?"

Calm down. You're okay. She's not a threat. It's just a question.

"The Maiden's Touch is being deployed in just a couple of days, and I've got to say," she leans in, whispering. "I don't have a good feeling about it, especially since we're all being forced to take it."

I scrutinize her. The steam rising from the pancakes clouds my glasses. "I don't like it either, but I guess there's really nothing we can do, you know?"

"Yeah, that's true." She glances back at her oldest daughter, who's working register. "I'm just. . . I don't know, sweetie. I'm just worried. No one in this once great country trusts, well, you know who."

I grade her words, analyzing her facial expressions. "Careful, Mrs. Chindin, you wouldn't want all that heard by the wrong person." I pause, only a couple of other customers in the store. "But I agree."

"Lazarus."

That one word gets my left hand to instinctively move to the pistol concealed in my pocket.

Beads of sweat form at my hairline.

She knows.
Danger.
Kill her.
Run.
Stop it... No, you're okay.
Kill.

"What about them?" My hand slithers around the handle.

"It doesn't do my heart any good that they were chased into hiding, and it's weird, the pictures of them that were up for months stopped broadcasting out of nowhere. Still no curfew reinstated, still no new executions, nothing. It's almost like the world went into some parallel universe where we can live in peace."

Don't trust her.
Kill.
Survive.
Must survive.
Stop being so jumpy. Calm down. She isn't your enemy. She's Suzy. She's like your mom.

"I've noticed that, too," I say, forcing my shoulders to relax as more rain splashes the window next to me. "Saints aren't monitoring any of the checkpoints, either. It's like we're in some sort of utopia."

It's because he wants us to drop our guard.

She continues, "Yeah, but anyway—" The door to the diner opens, and in walks another customer. Suzy turns away to face the patron. "Good morning, Liz!" she glances back, smiling. "I'll see you tomorrow, Michael."

"Yep, see ya." I almost whisper. I let go of my gun.

Paranoia. The fear of getting caught. A Saint, Reaper, or even Robyn could be hiding behind the corner just waiting for the right moment to strike.

I don't sleep. I know that doesn't help.

I should've made sure Robyn was incapable of coming back.

Those Saints. If only they would've pulled up a minute later, I wouldn't have to worry about that freak lurking in the shadows. I know she's back. She must be. Mills wouldn't let his play thing stay dead.

I stare down at the pancakes in front of me. Frozen, my fork hovers above the plate. Every time I try to take a bite, my hand seizes up, and I groan. I have to convince myself that they aren't laced. The inner argument takes longer than usual, but I eventually smear butter and syrup over them.

I force my fork through the food and cautiously dig in.

※

I'M DRENCHED, STEPPING ONE FOOT IN FRONT OF THE other, passing small houses and businesses. The distance between me and the cemetery decreases.

The wind attempts to rip a flyer free from one of the stop signs. It shows a picture of a gorgeous woman standing in a field of sunflowers. There's a bunch of words beneath it. I already know what it says:

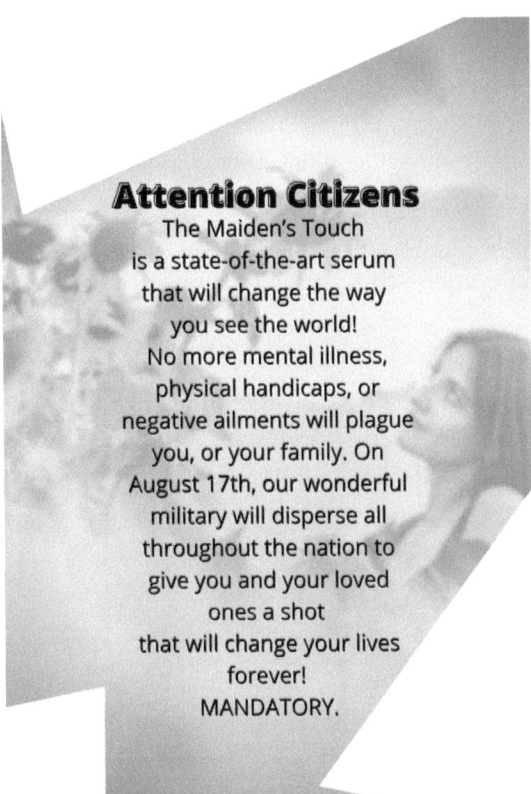

Attention Citizens
The Maiden's Touch
is a state-of-the-art serum
that will change the way
you see the world!
No more mental illness,
physical handicaps, or
negative ailments will plague
you, or your family. On
August 17th, our wonderful
military will disperse all
throughout the nation to
give you and your loved
ones a shot
that will change your lives
forever!
MANDATORY.

I've seen it over a hundred times. They're posted on every street corner, bus stop, etc.

Mills was smart to portray his serum this way, and I hate that. In three days, anyone who isn't *perfect* will be killed by the poison that is injected into their veins, and the rest will become immortal, forced to breed for the President until they've outlived their usefulness.

I found a flash drive on Dante's body the night I buried him. I plugged it into one of the laptops at the library, and I was relieved to see that it was an encrypted communication app he was using to talk to Cass. Problem is, I've checked the app every single day for the past five months, and nothing.

Our only hope of overthrowing the government seems to be dead.

Gone.

I can't even imagine what they probably did to Cass. An enslavement camp where the women are treated like toys to reward the slaves that gather resources.

I shudder, approaching the black metal gates that guard the cemetery

I'm sorry, Cass.

I pass through the entrance, the rain falling even harder now. I trudge to the back of the field next to an oak tree. My lungs feel compressed, heavy, just like all the other days I come to visit.

Their graves aren't marked. I stop where I buried them, allowing a sigh to escape my mouth. I hope that it will relieve the pressure I feel in my chest. It doesn't.

"Hey," I say. The leaves on the tree shelter me from some of the rain. "Sorry. I'm a bit later than usual."

Dante and Raphael don't say anything, but I don't care.

I stare at the blades of grass that cover them. The words tumble from my lips, "Three more days, then I'll see you guys again."

No reply.

"I think I'm ready, but I guess that doesn't matter." I focus on Raph's grave. "I know I've told you this a hundred times, but I was trying to run away before you left us. I was going to go live *happily ever after* with Chloe while you and the others saved us all. Selfish, I know. The guilt won't leave because I never got the chance to confess that to you when you were alive."

The sounds of rain and wind wrap around me as I talk to them. I tell them about my paranoia, and how I can't sleep all that well. I apologize for all the inconveniences that I may have caused, and last, I ask them what it's like to be dead.

I try to do this every day, because when I die, I would want someone to do the same for me.

Death is an introvert, encasing his victims in loneliness.

The loneliness cripples me with fear.

Clear tears trickle down my cheeks. The long-lasting side effect of Rebirth is gone now.

My nose runs. "Why the hell did you pick me?" I ask, dropping to my knees and tucking my chin. "Why couldn't you have just left me to die with mom and dad? I hate this. I *hate* being here, and it's all your fault. You should've killed me back in Boston when I ran away. When you found me at the funeral, you should've slit my throat, or put a bullet in my twisted head!"

I grit my teeth. My ears are buzzing as more tears escape my eyes

Still, there's no reply.

"Now look where we are. . . Chloe is in a land of make believe where she thinks we're actually married with no care in the world, and Blaine drinks more than an abusive stepdad."

I stay on my knees. The wet grass soaks my clothes further.

Listening to the raindrops splash against the leaves above, I force myself to breathe. "I'm sorry. I don't really mean all of that, I don't think. I'm just trying to be okay. I'm trying to look on the bright side. I'll get to see my mom and dad, you, Simon, Mae, Tommy, Marcy, and everybody else. I won't be in pain anymore, and I'll finally be able to rest."

My own words startle me as they leave my mouth. The thought of being killed and left to rot in the middle of the street as immortal beings bare children into the world to worship Mills makes my skin crawl.

I imagine maggots burrowing their way into my flesh, eating my body until its nothing but a decayed corpse. I imagine wild dogs roaming the cities for food. They'd stumble upon my decomposing figure and take bites out of my face, growling with delight as I feed their starving bellies.

I violently shake my head to empty the image from my mind, getting to my feet.

Some of the fog that was clouding my mind dissipates. A sense of clarity washes over me.

I don't think anything is wrong with Chloe. So, if she was injected, she would become an immortal and enslaved by that psychopath.

I picture him grabbing her thighs, his boney fingers creeping beneath her clothing.

"No. . . No, I'm not done, yet," I mutter, my breathing labored. "I'm not going out like this, like some whinny prick who can't help himself. I'm not going to end up like you two. Not yet."

I turn from their graves, the blood in my body rushing through every vein, my lust for murder rising yet again.

I'm going to kill them all.

CHAPTER SIXTEEN

Trees stay anchored in the ground as the wind forces them to bend to its will. The large blue house at the end of the street gets closer.

I have soaked clothes and chattering teeth.

Angels weep above.

The front lawn soaks my shoes, then my socks.

You're the only one who can do this. The only one who can win. I guess I'm trying to convince myself more than anyone else.

My hand covers the doorknob, but it refuses to turn when twisted.

A sigh leaves my mouth. Reaching into my right pocket, I pull out a set of keys, scanning through each of them until I find a silver one with the number *two* printed on it.

"Here we go," I mumble, inserting the key and unlocking the door.

The house has a strong scent of cinnamon. None of the lights are on, and since there's nothing but gloom outside, I reach for the nearest switch to drive it out with electricity.

The living room lights up.

"Chloe?" My shadow glides across the furniture on my way to the kitchen. "Hello? Are you in—"

"Surprise!" She jumps out with Blaine at her side.

I jump but quickly regain my composure. Decorations adorn the place, and a blue banner wishes someone a happy birthday. "What's all this?"

Chloe smiles with a laugh, "Did you forget what today was, dummy?"

The violent thoughts I was projecting moments before are shoved aside as I try to remember the mundane, "Oh. . . That's today?"

Blaine snorts. His eyes lack the optimism they once held. "Ah, big nineteen. Good thing you have us to remind you, dudezo."

Chloe points to the girly little party hat on his head. "Look what I made him wear."

I smirk. "It's pretty."

He glares. "Oh, I'll show you pretty."

We both laugh.

My bloodlust fights within me to overpower other emotions.

"Listen," I say. The vibe in the room instantly changes. "The three of us need to talk."

"Not now." Chloe motions to some cupcakes on the counter. "You gotta eat those first."

Blaine walks past me, opening the freezer and pulling out a bottle of vodka. "Yeah, she frosted them herself."

My foot taps against the floor. Too many thoughts battle each other. "Okay, we can talk after."

Chloe looks me up and down, "Are you okay?"

"Yeah." I lean on the counter, choosing between chocolate and vanilla. Vanilla wins. "I just had a bit of a wakeup call."

Blaine takes a swig of vodka straight out of the bottle. "A bit late for that, don't you think? What, with all of us dying here in a couple of days."

His pessimism almost causes me to roll my eyes. I open my mouth to take a bite out of my desert.

"Hey, wait," Chloe interrupts, frowning. "We didn't sing you happy birthday, yet."

"Oh." I lower the cupcake from my mouth, swallowing the saliva it produced. "Sorry."

"It's cool, just chill." She nudges Blaine, who's taking another swig. "Come on."

He sighs, stepping forward, bottle in hand. "Fine."

They both sing to me, purposefully sounding stupid to make me laugh.

It works.

"Okay, okay," she chuckles. "Now you can eat."

I take a bite. It tastes amazing. "Store bought?"

"Nah, from scratch."

"So, that's why you didn't come to breakfast this morning."

"Bingo."

Blaine butts in, "Just so you know, I helped clean after she was done."

The three of us keep the conversation light while we eat the cupcakes. An occasional strike of lightning and bit of thunder shakes the house. After we're finished, I take them into the living room where we all sit down.

Rain spatters against the windows.

Blaine leans back in a recliner. "So, what's this *wakeup call* you wanted to talk about?"

I carefully consider which words to use. "It's just us. . . we're all that's left."

"Ah, depressing."

"Blaine," Chloe interjects.

"Sorry." He sheepishly takes a swig of his bottle.

I continue, "I was at the cemetery this morning, and thought of rotting away as Mills started the world over again. It made me sick to my stomach. I know Cass is probably dead, but there has to be one last failsafe to shut this whole thing down."

Chloe bites her tongue.

"What?" I ask.

Her mouth opens, but she doesn't say anything for a while. "You're right, there is only three of us left. We have a few weapons upstairs, and a few boxes of ammo, but that isn't enough to stop this."

Our logics clash. "All we have to do is get the people on our side."

"How?" Blaine asks. He sets the vodka down on an end table next to him. "They're scared, too. At least we have guns. All they have are their bare hands and maybe a screwdriver from their shed."

"We— ugh, I don't know. But I don't want to just sit here and wait for two Reapers to show up at our door and either recognize who we are and gun us down or inject us with the Maiden's Touch. I don't know about Chloe, but you and I have plenty of genetic imperfections, man. I have dyslexia, and you're an *albino*."

"Fair point."

Chloe chews her bottom lip. "Okay, but you still haven't offered up any ideas on how we can get everyone angry enough to rise up. If they haven't already, it's going to take something big. Without Cass, that's kinda impossible."

"I—" my mind going blank. "You're right, but there has to be something."

"Look." Her voice calms me. "After Raphael died, you became our leader. Whatever you say, we'll do. Just please be smart about it."

"Be smart?" Blaine's face lacks any sort of emotion. "The worst he can do is get us killed, which is going to happen regardless of if we do anything at all."

His words ironically encourage me. "Exactly."

Chloe leaks a little smile. She stands from the couch and puts her hand on my shoulder. "Well, okay then. Here. Before we try to save the world, you and I are going on a walk, birthday boy."

"You know it's raining like crazy out there, right?"

"Come on."

"You're the boss."

I close my fingers around hers.

CHAPTER SEVENTEEN

The woods. A perfect place for a romantic walk or tossing a corpse.

Cheshire is out of sight to most of the world. Secluded. The still scenery is calming but come nightfall it's kind of hard to forget the horror stories Simon used to tell me when we were kids.

"You sure you didn't take me out here to kill me?" I chuckle.

"Who knows?" She nudges me. "This *would* be a good place to do it if I were."

A flowing creek trickles next to us as we walk down the wet trail. A toad croaks from a water lily. The smell of moss and wet wood fill my nose.

We've been walking for a little under an hour. We're drenched, but my thoughts are clear, my step is light, and there's nowhere else my soul wishes to be.

Her presence is always enough. When she's around, there's normality, a sense of stability.

"We don't really talk much about our lives before Lazarus," she mentions. "What was a normal day for you before you were, well, you know?"

"A wanted terrorist?" It's impossible not to laugh. I step over a puddle. "Well, I was about to graduate when I was executed. I lived over in Brookhaven. You ever heard of it?"

"Oh, that rich kid subdivision?"

"Not all of us were rich."

"Uh-huh, sure. That's why there was a huge mansion in the backwoods were all the popular kids would party, right?"

"I went there maybe twice, and both times, death stalked the place. Plus, like I said, not *all* of us had money. I mooched off my friends whenever I could, and my parents both worked."

"Whatever you say. Now go on. What else?"

"Well, it was always just me and Simon—oh, and his girlfriend, Julie. The three of us didn't really have a crowd, so we stuck together and made our own."

"So, you three were a bunch of losers?"

"Nah, not really. We weren't super popular, but we definitely weren't corner kids."

"Corner kids?"

"You know. Outcasts. Socially awkward kids who smelled like they hadn't taken a shower in two weeks and needed to go to therapy because they couldn't get rid of their stuffed animals without crying."

"That's oddly specific."

"Yeah, well there were definitely a few cases at Lakeshore."

"Well, what did you do for fun?"

"Dumb stuff."

"Such as?"

"I dunno, sneaking into my dad's wine cabinet, watching horror movies." The memories force a smile to escape. "Snorting candy dust on New Year's Eve."

"Candy dust? So, you *were* lame."

"What? Just because I didn't do the real stuff like you, that makes me lame?"

She laughs, "Hey, just because I lived in Collingsworth doesn't mean I used drugs. I only kinda hung around the ones who did. It's like I told you, I was with a bad crowd after my dad passed away. All we ever did was hookup with boys and steal stuff for money."

"Hookup?" The word leaves my mouth dry. "What do you mean by that?"

A smug grin appears across her face. "Oh, what? You jealous?"

"Depends on your definition of *hooked up*."

She rolls her eyes, giggling. "You were my first kiss. My so-called *friends* were the ones sleeping around and being degenerates." She reaches for my hand. "One guy did try to get with me once, though."

"Oh yeah?"

"Yeah, he was playing it pretty smooth before he grabbed my butt."

"And how did that go for him?"

"I broke his hand. Dude's may be stronger, but when you aren't expecting someone to twist your wrist, you guys are pretty easy to break."

"That's cute."

"What is?"

"You were rough around the edges."

"And that's cute?"

"Yeah, kinda."

"You're dumb."

We stop on a little wooden bridge that crosses the little brook. The view is breathtaking, unlike anything I've ever really seen before. It feels untouched by the world, thriving in its natural state.

"Ah, our first kiss. Wasn't it romantic?" she asks suddenly.

I can't tell if she's being sarcastic or not.

I take a deep breath, suppressing my chuckle. "Nothing screams *romantic* like kissing in a bathroom after I just murdered my childhood bully."

"Hey, the tie you wore was super nice."

The rain falls harder. A flash of lightening sparks across the gloomy sky.

We keep walking.

Random thoughts spark through my mind and I shoot out a nagging question. "Have you ever wondered where Rebirth came from?"

"Not really. I'm pretty sure Lazarus was the only group that knew about it, but then White raided all the facilities and took it for the government... Maybe Vice created it?"

"Vice was insane. I doubt he could create a serum that brings the dead back to life."

"Wait... I remember Raphael talking about it in Salem when we were tortured together."

"Really? What did he say?"

"Something about Vice having a wife who worked for Mills as a scientist, and how she and a lab buddy of hers made a break though in reconstructive science... at least, I think—"

"I never heard about this."

"He was doped up pretty bad when he started spilling his guts."

"What else did he say about her?"

"That she was going to show the world what she created, but Mills wanted it kept secret, so he had her assassinated."

"And then?"

"Vice went mad. He broke into her office, took all her notes and research, destroyed the prototype the government had, and finished her work while also forming Lazarus."

"You know, for being his heir and all, he really should've given me all the backstory."

"Is it really that important?"

"I guess not."

More lightning shoots across the sky followed by thunder.

"So." She squeezes my hand a little. "When are you going to propose?"

I spit out my imaginary drink, stopping dead in my tracks. My face burns. "What?"

Her eyes lighten up, "Oh, what, are we just going to go our separate ways after we overthrow Mills?"

"No, no, I'm just. . . you want me to marry you? Like, for real?"

She shrugs. "Well, only if you want to."

I don't know what to say. Despite the cold, my body feels shrouded in flames. "Well, of course I do— well, I mean—"

She punches my shoulder. "You're so nervous. It's adorable."

"You're mean."

"It's been fun being your pretend wife all these months, *Mr. Valentine*. I definitely wouldn't mind the real thing one day. That is, if we don't get murdered or poisoned in the next three days."

I raise an eyebrow. "Have we ever even made *us* official?"

"Well, between getting sent on a suicide mission, getting into a car crash and you going into a coma, being locked up in Salem, almost being beheaded, serving as slaves inside the President's manor, destroying a biochemical weapon, me being kidnapped, all our friends dying, and an impending mass genocide, I don't think we've really found the time."

"We've been through a lot, haven't we?"

"Yeah, enough crap to last a lifetime."

"We could always make it official now, you know?" I shrug.

"In the middle of a forest in rural Massachusetts while a killer storm is soaking us through our clothes?"

"Precisely."

"You can totally see my bra," she giggles.

"I wasn't even looking."

"You sure?"

"Not intentionally."

"Hmm."

"Do you want to make it official, or not?"

She smiles. "Go for it."

Even though our love is obvious, my throat threatens to close. "Will you be my girlfriend?"

"No."

"Wow."

"You could always beg."

"Beg?"

"Yeah, like a dog."

"Do you get off on teasing me?"

"A little."

"Happy birthday to me."

"Aww, stop. Of course, I'll be your girlfriend. I already have been."

"I know, I know."

Her smile gets bigger. We kiss. She doesn't let go, and we keep our lips pressed.

She wraps her arms around my shoulders. I put my hands on her waist. I've never been this happy. I'm awake and aware. My mind finally lets itself slow down a bit.

When we part, I look at her red face.

"Come on, we've got one last thing to do," Chloe says.

"Which is?"

"Just come on."

She grabs me by the hand and leads me further down the trail, eventually stopping in front of a bunch of small rocks next to the creek. She squats down and studies each of them, picking a cool one and holding it out for me.

"A rock?" I ask. It's silver with streaks of red etched in it.

"Yeah, a rock. A relationship rock, and you'll always keep it in your pocket for good luck. It'll remind you that I care about you and gushy relationship stuff like that."

I put the keepsake in my pocket then squat down. I study each of the pretty pieces of nature, eventually finding a smooth beige rock. I put it in her hand.

Her smile is larger than life. She puts it away and hugs me.

A loud chirp sounds from my back pocket. We jump in unison. I retrieve the flash drive I took from Dante.

It's flashing orange.

Chloe and I exchange looks before running into town like our lives depend on it.

Because they do.

CHAPTER EIGHTEEN

"Oh, Mr. and Mrs. Valentine." Opel Reed, the librarian, greets us as we rush through the doors. "I was just about to lock up for the night."

"Emergency." We pass her with a shout. "We'll be out in just a few."

"Oh, okay." She lets out a little annoyed squeak but says nothing else.

We enter the computer room. I sit down at one of the laptops, and Chloe finds a chair and pulls it up next to me. I practically shove the flash drive into an open slot, taking my glasses off and tossing them in my lap.

An application opens on screen. It's orange, and a message pops up.

"Transmission loading," Chloe answers before I can ask.

The screen transitions to a room made of metal. Body bags litter the floor, piled up on top of each other, smothering the space from the area. Cass sits in front of the screen, her face paler than ever. Her white tank top is shredded, and there's black blood gushing from a wound in her shoulder.

The door behind her is barricaded with a table. Someone's pounding on it, demanding to be let in.

"Dante, I did it." Her voice is weak, her pupils abnormally wide. "I got the footage, but. . . you don't need to come back for me." She coughs black into her elbow. "One of the victims got their blood in my mouth, and the poison is already eating away at my brain. I uploaded the footage into the app. Download it onto your drive then erase everything else. I was infected a few hours ago. . . wait, maybe it's been a day. . . I'm starting to lose it. I can feel the poison dissolving my mind—"

The banging gets louder. A few muffled gunshots ring out from behind.

"The weakness for the immortals is what you suspected it to be. An EMP. But in case you were wondering, no, it doesn't work if you try to use it on a genetically imperfect person." She stops as more shots pop off. Her lungs deflate. "Listen, I don't have much time. I need to be quick with my words." She coughs once more before flashing the camera a small monitor attached to her wrist. "I programmed the laptop to wipe itself along with the flash drive after my heartbeat stops, that way they won't be able to track you—"

"*Open the damn door, Cass!*" someone screams off screen.

I chew my cheek. She picks a handgun up off the floor. It's prerecorded. What's done is done.

"Thank you for showing me that life could be so much more than just suffering in a grim society, Dante." She pushes the barrel against her temple. Black tears stream down her face. "Tell the others that I'm grateful for them, and please. . . please don't let this be for nothing."

She pulls the trigger just as the door behind her is forced open.

The table is flung aside by two Saints who storm the room. One of them swears at the bloody sight, and the other eyes the screen. "She's sending all the footage to Lazarus!"

The first pulls at his ski mask, sweat pouring down his frame. "Shut it down!"

He rushes to the laptop, but before he can touch it, the monitor on Cass's wrist chirps, and the screen goes black.

We stare with lowered jaws. Our screen transitions to a file folder with two items in it.

"The first file is labeled *Total Chaos* and the second is the transmission we just watched," Chloe whispers.

"I'm going to download both of them," I say.

Both files are dragged into the export folder and downloaded. I then erase the application from the drive and pull it from the laptop.

"We have it," she says, her disbelief fading. "We actually have it."

"I know." A foreign emotion rises in my chest. "We should get back to the house."

"Yeah, let's go."

Mrs. Reed opens the door to the computer room. A frown is pasted on her face. With glassy eyes, she asks, "Can you two maybe finish this tomorrow? I'm going to miss my granddaughter's play."

"Y-yeah, sorry about that, ma'am," I apologize.

Chloe clears her throat. "Could we maybe borrow this laptop if we promise to bring it back?"

She looks around like she's being watched. "I don't know. . . it's against policy."

"Please? It's urgent." I put the rain-speckled glasses back on my face.

Mrs. Reed sighs, "Oh, all right. Just please be careful with it."

We agree, getting out of our chairs.

"Thank you so much," I say.

Chloe grabs the laptop.

The two of us rush out of the library. The feeling in my chest continues to rise. I don't recognize it, so I have to search for the name that best describes it.

It gets stronger, demanding attention.

Hope.

CHAPTER NINETEEN

Our energy feeds each other. Entering the house, I could run a marathon.

"Blaine!" Dopamine. Sweet, sweet dopamine. "Blaine, we've got it!"

"Oh." Chloe stares into the living room. "He's blacked out, again."

I make my way to the recliner. Blaine's leaned back with an empty vodka bottle on the floor next to him.

"He's going to drink himself to death," I mutter.

"Not when he finds out we just fixed everything."

With a smile, I say, "That's true."

She moves closer, placing the laptop on the end table, "Here, help me get him up to bed."

I grab his legs, she grabs his arms, and the two of us haul his limp body up to the second floor.

"He's heavier than he looks," Chloe grunts, taking another step backward.

"He had nothing to do but workout for five years. Dude's pure muscle."

We get him to the top of the landing, making a left into his bedroom before tossing him onto his mattress.

Chloe tucks him in with a blanket.

"You're such a mom," I chuckle.

She narrows her eyes. "Am not."

"Are too."

She untucks him. "How 'bout now?"

I laugh, letting it echo off the walls.

Puke suddenly gushes out from Blaine's lips.

"Ah, damn it!" I turn him on his side. My nose stings from the smell.

Chloe groans, "You idiot. I'm not letting you drink anymore."

He doesn't reply. His mattress is covered in his vomit. I contemplate pushing him onto the floor.

"Screw it." Grabbing him by the foot, I drag him off the mattress. "He can stay in my bed."

"Where will you sleep?"

"I don't know, I guess the couch."

I wanted to say *Your room?*, but whenever the subject rises, I get sheepish.

His body slogs through the doorway, across the hall, and into my room. We near my bed and Chloe assists getting him situated. Now sprawled out over my comforter, his face rolls to the side.

"You better not puke in my bed, Blaine." I smack him on the arm. He answers me with a snort.

My face itches. I scratch the hair that covers my cheek. "Hey, do you gotta razor?" I ask Chloe.

"Yeah, why? You finally gonna shave?"

"Probably. I don't think I need to look like this anymore."

"Does that mean I can stop wearing that stupid wig when we go out?"

"You really hate it, don't you?"

"Insanely."

"I think it looks cute."

She frowns. "Cuter than my real hair?"

"Pfft, no. Nothing beats a natural blond."

"Good. Here, let's go get you that razor."

She escorts me from my room to her own. It's bigger than the others. We enter the bathroom. She reaches into one of her drawers, pulling out a pink razor along with some girly shaving cream.

"Sorry, I'm sure you don't want to smell like. . ." She gazes at the label. ". . .honey blossoms and sugar cubes, but it's all I have."

"It's fine."

She steps past me to her bed, "Come talk to me when you're done, 'kay?"

I nod, and then focus my attention on the image in the mirror. My beard isn't long and gross or anything, it just isn't me. It makes me appear way older, and I already looked older than nineteen from the get-go.

I take the cap off her shaving cream and smear some of the gel across my face. Then, I pull the razor down my left cheek.

When I was fifteen, my dad taught me how to shave without nicking myself.

"Like this, Jay," he said, demonstrating.

"But my face feels like sandpaper after," I bitched, pressing my razor down my face.

"Then you're not doing it right."

"Whatever, dad."

My lungs deflate. Eventually, I look like myself, again.

The glasses on my face give me an intense recollection of life before Lazarus. I can't decide whether I like the look or not. There isn't even a prescription in it since my vision was fixed after being brought back.

I don't think I like being reminded of my old life.

Before Lazarus, I was naïve and stupid. There wasn't a care in the world. All I wanted to do was have fun with nobody in my business.

To think, if I was never executed, I would have died from the God Code, or, if not that, the Maiden's Touch. My life was bound to change regardless of my family's execution.

Change.

I hate that word.

Good things change. They always do.

Mills has always made sure for of that.

I know I wanted to leave with Chloe and never look back, but I had lost sight of what mattered most. Killing Matthew was never my release. Revenge was great, sure, but it didn't change a thing. Another person took his place, and the horror show that is this life went on. Matthew was a diabolical human being who I hope is rotting in hell, but his existence, everything he ever amounted to be, was nothing compared to Mills. He's the real threat, the real reason why things are the way they are.

I'll kill him. I'll be the winner.

Not him.

Me.

Today, the total member count in Lazarus is three, but tomorrow. . . millions.

I finish rinsing my face, taking my glasses off and putting them in one of the drawers along with her stuff. I enter her room. She's reading a book.

"Whatcha got there?" I ask.

"Ah, you look great. I forgot how much I liked seeing your face." She pauses. "Oh, and I'm just reading this dumb self-help guide."

"Oh, sounds thrilling."

"It is. You can give it a read when I'm done."

"That would probably take me a good couple months."

"Hey, that's only if you're stressed. You read things pretty quick when you aren't under pressure."

"I mean, sure, but with what's going on, I doubt that'll be anytime soon." I move to the closed door. "Well, anyway, I guess

I'll go make a bed on the couch. Thank you for making my birthday so special. I really loved those cupcakes."

"Really? It was my first time making something from scratch. I was worried you were going to hate it."

"Hate it? It tasted just like my mom's."

"Dude, that makes me feel so much better."

I smile, reaching for the knob. "I'm glad—"

"Hey, wait." She stops me. "You don't have to go."

"Huh? What do you mean?"

"Nothing really, I'm just cold."

My ears burn. "Wait, are you—"

"Shut up. You don't have to. I'm just saying, it'll be more comfortable than the couch."

Her blush is contagious. "Are you sure?"

"I wouldn't have brought it up if I wasn't. It's been five months, and you're too shy to make the first move."

Her blond hair is up in a messy bun. She's changed out of her wet clothes, and now wears a baggy t-shirt and shorts.

Love. Your brain goes numb. Our Lips touch and fingers become intertwined. She's everything.

We part. Her gorgeous green eyes wrap me in a comfortable embrace.

Home.

"What?" She smiles.

"I love you," I say.

She giggles, sedately leaning in. "I love you, too."

We kiss.

I don't want it to stop. I lower her to the bed, stroking her cheek.

She bites my lip. My heart pounds.

Sliding a hand up the back of my shirt, her warm fingertips trail along my shoulder blades.

Heat spreads down my body. My other hand inches under her shirt, grasping her hip.

We met in combat class well over a year ago. Who could have guessed this would be us? That we'd suffer together like this? She's my other half. Sometimes I forget she's a real person and not just a perfect figment of my damaged imagination.

Without her, there is no me.

Another flash of lightning flashes outside the window.

The storm seems like it will never end.

Our breathing becomes heavy.

CHAPTER TWENTY

The sun outside slowly rises as I sluggishly enter my room. "*Psst.*" My feet drag toward Blaine. There's a gross amount of dried puke on his chin. "Hey, wake up."

He jerks awake, groaning, "What do you want, Raph?"

I inch closer. "It's Jason."

He blinks a few times, sitting up. "Oh, sorry, man, I—"

My hand raises. "It's fine, dude."

He blinks some more and looks around. "Why am I in your room?"

"Because you puked all over your bed."

"Wait, then where did you sleep? The flo—" He stops and scrutinizes my messy hair and bags beneath my eyes. "Oh, you didn't." A stupid grin sweeps across his face. "You *didn't.*"

Don't smile.

Don't.

My lips curl.

Crap.

"Aaaah! Let's go!" He pumps his fist.

"Shut up."

He laughs, "My baby boy's growing up."

"Literally, shut up."

"Man, if only Raphael was here to see this." Registering what was just said, his grin fades. "He'd probably get a good laugh out of it or tell you two to focus on our mission."

"You wanna make him proud?"

"What do you mean?"

"Cass. . . she sent the footage over last night. All we have to do is break into one of the broadcasting buildings and stream it to everyone."

His jaw drops. "You're kidding."

"No, Chloe's getting dressed, then we're leaving."

He flings himself out of bed. "Crap, ah, ah—" he shields his eyes and stops in his tracks "Hangover."

"Your own fault."

"Oh really? I didn't know that."

"Need me to get you anything?"

"No, just some help downstairs. Food usually helps."

I support his weight, taking him downstairs and into the kitchen where he sits after snatching some deli meat from the fridge and potato chips from one of the cupboards.

"I lied," he says, devouring the meat. "Could you actually go get my shades from the living room?"

"Yeah, sure."

When I get back, we discuss what we want to do after all this is over. He used to jokingly say he would get into comedy, but he's not the same guy. Since the night Raph and Dante died, all that remains of Blaine is a twisted shell of his former self. All he does is drink, sleep, repeat.

I don't blame him. I don't even blame myself anymore.

It was Mills. I'm tired of blaming anyone else.

My parents' death? His fault.

My death? His fault.

Simon's death? His fault.

Dante and Raphael's death? His fault.

Chloe enters the kitchen. She holds the laptop. "Okay, so I did some looking around."

"And?" I ask.

She turns the screen toward us. She shows us an aerial shot of a secluded building with a large satellite dish installed on the roof.

"There's three buildings like this throughout the country. One in Texas, one in Seattle, and one in Boston. They're the only places that can receive and stream mass broadcasts."

"Convenient." Blaine shoves a handful of chips in his mouth.

"Mhmm, now unless you want to travel to Texas, I think it's safe to say we'll hit the one in Boston."

I study the image. "There's a checkpoint on every side of the building. Strong military presence. Makes sense."

Blaine groans, "Do we have to dress up like soldiers again? I hate when I can't wear my shades."

"We've played that card too many times. We need to get in by different means," I say.

Chloe sets the laptop down on the kitchen counter. "We could hit them with a car bomb and rush in before they even know what's going on?"

Blaine shakes his head. "We don't have any C4, and hitting a weapons armory and stealing some would be a bad idea right before a raid."

"He's right." I tap my cheek. "I think a stealthy approach would be our best bet."

"We'd have to kill them all," Chloe notes, snatching one of Blaine's chips. "Because if we leave any alive, they'll swarm in and possibly interrupt us while the footage streams and shut it down."

"We could pick them off one by one while Jason sneaks in and takes care of the upload?" Blaine suggests.

Chloe points. "Yeah, we should do that."

"What if the footage isn't enough?" Cynicism is my forte.

"I thought you might ask that." She steals another chip.

"Hey! Stop stealing my crap, you bimbo," Blaine teases.

"In the broadcasting room, there should be a camera that you can connect to the stream. You could tell everyone what we're fighting for."

"Cringe," Blaine mutters.

"It's not cringe," she argues.

I leave my chair. "Sounds like we have a plan. Let's get all our crap together. Remember, we only have a couple hundred rounds of ammo left, so try to use your knives."

CHAPTER TWENTY-ONE

The grass beneath my feet is soggy. I trudge through the flooded lawn while the trees around me sway violently. The howling wind is blocked from stinging my face with the help of the mask. It's the same mask I wore during the raid at the God Code facility. All the carnage that took place that night threatens to tarnish my vision, but I've grown numb to it.

Violence doesn't bother me.

Sometimes, I enjoy it.

I'm wearing the Lazarus uniform, which keep my identity hidden and my body protected. Everything vital is covered, so if I'm shot, I won't be mortally wounded. Maybe. We're in the end game.

"It's almost go time." Chloe leans up against a tree. She's dressed identical to me. "Are you two ready for this?" she asks.

Blaine gives a thumbs up. "More than ready. These dickheads are finally going pay for what they've done."

"Payback's a bitch," I mutter.

The backpack slung over my shoulders houses the flash drive and a few other things.

I gaze at the massive satellite dish that rotates atop the

building ahead. Lightning flashes above, and despite that, it's darker than normal. It's been raining for days on end. It gives us the advantage.

Louder.

Darker.

I adore Mother Nature, especially on nights like these.

"I probably don't have to say this," I start. "But there's three of us, and who knows how many of them. Like I said back at the house, use your knives in all circumstances possible."

"We know," Blaine interrupts. "Trust me, being reckless isn't on my mind, right now."

Chloe steps away from the tree, wrapping her fingers around my forearm. "If you get in there and there's too many of them, don't be stupid. Lure them away one by one, and we'll be in as soon as the outer guards are dead."

I nod.

Blaine steps past me, taking a deep breath. "All right, let's do this."

They step into the darkness, crouched down and creeping forward like predators.

I keep my position and watch with vigilant eyes.

Now is the only time we have, and the only time we have any control over.

I SNEAK PAST THE UN-GUARDED ENTRANCE, STICKING to the shadows. With my night vision on, I spot a sniper on the roof. He isn't taking his job too seriously, but that'll change if he sees me or any of the dead bodies that have been dragged into the dark.

There are no signs of Chloe or Blaine, but no gunshots have gone off, assuring me it's mostly safe.

I sneak past the blinding light above and see two ways of entry.

The double doors ahead of me, or a window to my left.

You'll run into soldiers if you use the front door, stupid.

I approach the window. I sink in the ground beneath. It's a muddy swamp.

Placing both palms on the glass, I push up. I'm surprised it's unlocked as I hoist myself through the window and into a small office. A small desk with a computer rests in the corner.

I carefully shut the window before creeping through the room and placing my ear up to the door.

Nothing. The storm outside demands to be heard, masking my presence.

I unsheathe my knife with my left hand and use my right to twist the knob, pushing the door open. I peer into the long and empty hallway before making my way down the corridor, moving slowly and attempting to tune out the storm and listen for any other noises such a creaks, footsteps, talking, or coughs.

It's eerily silent.

Almost too silent.

Switching off my night vision, I make my way through the building, creeping through a maze of hallways and doors. Just as I'm opening a third pair of double doors, a loud chirp of a walkie-talkie goes off beyond the dense oak.

I put my ear up against the door.

"Echo five, this is Bravo four, do you read?"

"Yes, we read."

"Outer team's gone dark. Boss man doesn't want any of us to leave our stations unless commotion is heard. Understood?"

"Understood. And by gone dark, do you mean *they* got to them?"

"Either that, or the storm is preventing communication. Since we're talking just fine, I assume it's the first so be on the lookout."

"Yes, sir."

"Bravo Four, out."

I pull my backpack off and reach inside, taking out a small device and clicking a button. The sound of a child crying bursts from its speakers, and I hug the nearest wall next to the doors.

"What the hell?" A Saint pushes through the entrance with his gun drawn.

The second the door shuts behind him, I lunge, sinking my blade into his throat. He struggles, but I take him to the floor, tearing my blade from his flesh and slicing his jugular.

I kill the noise, shutting the device off.

Hurry, before more come.

I toss the corpse off me and get to my feet, opening one of the doors ever so slightly. Peeking through, I scan a lobby accompanied by a receptionist desk, waiting area, vending machines, more hallways that branch off, and a staircase in the back. Most importantly, five other Saints stand poised, frozen in the middle of the room. They stare at the doors I'm peering through.

"Fischer?" one of them calls, stepping forward. "You good?"

Think fast.

I step away from the doors and again reach into my backpack, pulling out another toy from Raph's stash. I mess with a few buttons on the small device, and after it's all dialed up, I abruptly kick the door open and toss.

Not even a second after it leaves my hand, the building goes black.

I reactivate my night vison as bullets riddle the door. I drop to the floor, holes punching through the wooden entrance and hallway walls.

Eventually, the gunfire ceases. I swing the backpack over my shoulders, scootching over to the damaged doors. I kick one of them open a second time.

More gunfire, but since I'm prone, my body remains unscathed as I crawl into the lobby.

The device I threw starts counting down from forty, warning me that my cover won't last long.

Getting to my feet, I silently step to the side of the room. The five Saints stand in formation, their sense of sight robbed from them. Their guns are aimed at the doors. None of them have spotted me.

"What's that thing counting down?" one asks.

"Shut up, Garner," another demands.

"What if it's a bomb?"

One of them nears the device and feels on the floor until he finds it, blindly tossing it as far as possible.

I creep forward. My knife is gripped in one hand, my pistol in the other.

"Twenty-five, twenty-four," the device chimes.

I rush in, stabbing a Saint through the cheek, shooting another in the throat.

All hell breaks loose.

I swat a gun out of the third's hand.

He headbutts me.

I blow his face apart.

Another tries to swing his rifle.

I stab him in the throat.

Ultimately, all five of them drop dead, collapsing at my feet.

I switch my night vision off.

"Two, one," the device chimes. The lights flicker back to life.

"Kill him!" a solider blurts from the top of the stairs. Two Saints charge down the steps.

One of them aims at me, but I'm quicker, shooting him twice.

His partner fires. The bullet catches me in the chest, hitting my Kevlar and knocking the wind out of me.

The sudden jolt is painful, but I still end his life with a bullet to the head.

I force myself to breathe, throwing myself toward the staircase.

It takes everything in me to keep my balance as each step takes me closer to my goal.

Inhale five seconds, exhale five seconds.

At the base of the stairs, I look up. Three more Saints rush for me. I instinctively shoot one in the leg. He crashes down the rest of the way. I kill a second, but a bullet hits my mask and makes my eardrums burst.

I fall backward, hitting the ground hard.

The pain is white hot, overwhelming to my senses. Still, it isn't enough to stop me from pulling the dirtiest trick in the book.

Playing dead.

I lie limp. The soldier clambers down the rest of the stairs.

He yells, "I got him! I got the bastard! He's dead!"

The Saint with a bullet in his leg groans by my side. "Could you celebrate a little later? I need help."

My alleged killer looks at his partner. "Don't worry, we're gonna get you help, Tyson."

He unhooks the radio from his belt, bringing it up to his mouth. "I got the intruder. Definitely a member of Lazarus. Boss, if you could head down here, we've got multiple casualties."

"Add another one." I lift my gun and shoot him in the head.

He collapses over me. His gore leaks across my mask.

I throw his corpse to the side, gradually getting to my feet. My head spins violently.

"No, no, please," the wounded Saint cries. Blood flows from his exposed leg. "I have a family. Please don't hurt me."

My vision is wavy. "You aren't worth the bullet."

A foot to the jaw puts him to sleep. More pain tremors through my head.

I rip my mask off. Nothing will stop the swirling. I blink, blink some more, then shake my head.

Bad idea.

I cringe, the pain even more prevalent. Again, my hands slither into my pack, and I pull out another item.

Aburaek. The pain numbing medication soldiers use to dull their infirmities.

I spill a couple pills into my palm and toss them in my mouth. After swallowing, I toss the bottle back in my pack and don my mask.

Please work quick like last time.

I gaze up the staircase to make sure more aren't coming, and after ejecting my magazine and pushing a new one into my gun, I make my way up the slippery steps.

CHAPTER TWENTY-TWO

Shooting, stabbing, breaking, kicking, killing. I fight my way through the building's second floor, ending the life of every soldier who stands in my way. It feels natural to me. With every throat that I slice, face that I shoot, arm that I snap, kneecap that I break, I'm forced to think that it was always supposed to be this way.

That I was destined to be a bringer of misery.

I clamber my way up a third set of stairs, my breathing heavy, my thoughts murderous. I get to the top step when a commotion breaks out from behind. I swing my gun around, ready to kill some more, but it's Chloe and Blaine.

"Remember guys, there's only three of us and who knows how many of them, so use your knives in every circumstance possible," Blaine mocks. "What happened to that, my good sir?"

I lower my weapon. "I did what I could."

"You're caked in blood. Are you hurt?" Chloe climbs the steps up to me.

I glance down at the scarlet dripping down my body. "This isn't mine."

She's opens her mouth to speak, but something falls in the distance.

The three of us go silent.

I face the noise, scrutinizing the scene ahead. A bunch of cubicles block any clear line of sight. There's only a small path between for people to walk. Near the back of the room, a staircase leads up to what I presume is the broadcasting room.

Blaine silently makes his way to our side, and we exchange looks, reading each other's minds.

Taking the lead, my gun is drawn and ready. They follow close behind. I'm less antsy with my back covered by the two people I trust most in the world.

Another crash echoes in the room. My gaze locks onto a bunch of bouncing pens that explode from one of the cubicles on the right.

Is someone trying to lure us in?

I step one foot closer, when a primal scream rings into the air.

A tall, grotesquely large Reaper barges out of the cubicle and rushes me. I fire four shots into him before he tackles me to the ground, his heavy frame crushing the air from my lungs as both my knife and pistol spring from my grip.

He wraps a meaty, gloved hand around my mask and rips it from my face.

Chloe shoots him in the neck, but it doesn't do anything. Black blood squirts from the wound.

An immortal.

He wraps one hand around my throat and uses the other to pry the gun out of Chloe's grip and hurl it at Blaine. It smacks him in the fingers, and he drops his weapon.

My eyes bulge as he squeezes my windpipe.

Chloe jumps on his back and tries put him into a blood choke, but he's too strong, using his free hand to grab her by the hair and yank her to the floor.

Blaine reaches for his gun, but the Reaper leans forward,

putting unbearable pressure on my neck. He grabs Blaine by the collar and smashes his face against the ground.

My vision darkens at the corners. I desperately reach for my knife, but it's just out of reach.

Chloe tries to get up.

The Reaper lets go of Blaine and slams his knuckles into her face.

She flies backward, smacking her head.

My teeth crush against each other. I use all my might to reach for my knife.

I reach.

And reach.

And reach.

It's as my eyes threaten to burst free from my skull when my fingers wrap around the handle. Taking the blade, I tear it across his wrist, spurting a fountain of black. His flesh is sawed away. He tries to punch me with his other hand, but Blaine stops him, taking his own knife and thrusting it through his throat.

He loosens his grip.

One last vicious slash of my blade.

His hand dangles from his wrist, and I'm able to twist to my side.

Chloe tackles him to the floor. She and Blaine throw devastating stabs and strikes.

I cough and fight for air.

Color returns to my vision. I get to my feet just in time for the Reaper to kick Blaine in the crotch and backhand Chloe hard enough to send her flying into one of the cubicles.

I grab my gun off the floor, hurling five rounds through his face.

He goes limp.

Chloe and I jump on the freak. We stomp his head until his mask falls apart and his skull caves.

She lowers herself to the floor. I put both arms behind my head, sucking in as much air as possible.

"Cheap-shot-hitting-bastard," Blaine groans on his knees.

My lips part, but a grotesque sound fills the air as black liquid shoots from what's left of the Reaper's face, forming the shape of a new one.

Chloe faces me. "Head to the broadcasting room and finish this. Blaine and I will hold him off."

Blaine groans some more. He spits on the floor. "Yeah, just hurry."

Without another word, I stumble to the stairs.

Gunshots ring out as Chloe insults the Reaper. I clamber up the steps. There's no stopping my invincibility.

I'm floating. On top of the world.

You're almost there.

Reaching the top, I jog down the only path, seeing twin doors at the back of the elongated hallway. It's all too surreal for me. I'm going to make it. I'm not going to die. I'm not going to be captured. . . An hour from now, the streets will be flooded with blood. It'll be an all-out war between us and the government.

The beginning of the end.

I think back to all the suffering in this nation, the lifetime of curfews, executions, lack of freedom. I've been robbed. Robbed of friends, family, normality, a chance at a decent life. Again, I guess that was never meant for me. It was always supposed to be like this.

In all things, there is opposition.

And when it comes down to Mills and his followers, that's what I am.

Opposition.

With a twist of a knob, I step into a room full of cameras, equipment, and computers. On the right, there's a large desktop with a tripod and camera next to the desk it's on. I force my feet to carry me there, and I peer at the sticky note placed on the keyboard.

With my mind at ease, I read, "Mass broadcast/streaming. Authorized accesses only."

I shake the mouse connected to the computer, waking it up. There's a password of course, but that won't stop me. I sling my backpack off my shoulders and set it down on the desk, pulling out a small device and plugging it into the computer.

The device hacks into the PC, bypassing all passwords and protection. Once it chimes at me, I unplug it and stick in back in the bag. Then, I pull out the flash drive with the footage on it.

Before plugging it in, I gaze at the few icons on the home screen. I find the one titled *Broadcast*. Clicking on the application, it boots up a screen that gives me two options.

Upload or stream.

I click upload, leading me to another screen that asks me to input a file. I comply.

More gunshots echo in the distance followed by yelling.

The sound is muted as I drag the file Cass made into the upload folder. A message pops up that reads, "Are you sure you want to broadcast this footage to every screen nationwide?"

Every fiber of my body erupts in euphoria.

Clicking yes, the screen goes black before switching to the film that will change everything.

Cass looks into the camera, sweeping her brown bangs out of her eyes. "My name is Cass. . . Cass Adams. I'm nineteen years old, and according to the president, I'm a terrorist, a monster who wants all of you seeing this to bow down to me, but that isn't true. I was a senior in high school when my family and I were murdered in our home for no reason other than not living up to Mills' standards. Lazarus, the organization that you've all been told to fear, brought me back from the dead and gave me a second chance—a chance that allowed me to gather the footage you're about to see and save you all from mass genocide."

The screen changes, showing the inside of a bright lab-like room with two men in white coats standing over a naked woman strapped to a gurney.

"Please," she cries. Her restraints prevent her thrashing. "I did everything I was told to do."

The man on the left ignores her, turning to the small cart by his side and lifting a syringe from its surface, "Why are you so distressed, Ms. Brown? You get to help further the research of our new serum. You're aiding God."

"He isn't God!" Her escape is futile. "Why me? Why are you doing this?"

The man on the right speaks, "Because you have autism. If that's the case, this should kill you."

She screams, a needle plunged through her flesh. Black liquid streams from her eyes, and she gasps.

The footage speeds up. Sometime later, the woman violently shakes as both men observe. They each write something down on their clipboards.

"Right on time," one says.

"We're getting consistent results. I think we can bring this to Finch."

The woman's liquefied brain flows out of her nose.

"How many do you think will be left to breed after deployment?"

"Well, considering that it'll eliminate anyone with a mental illness or physical defect, I'd say not too many, but more than enough. All we really need is two, but the more, the merrier."

"It's insane. Even if you have bad eyesight, it'll turn your brain to mush."

"People with disabilities have no room in the new world."

"Isn't your wife bipolar?"

"Your point?"

"Heh."

The scene switches to a compilation of women being abused

by soldiers and other slaves, men having their heads blown to pieces, and animals being tortured. Numerous people are injected with the Maiden's Touch before dying in horrific manners. This goes on for a few minutes, and the scene switches once again.

This time, it shows the inside of an office. It's clean and devoid of clutter. A desk and bookshelf are the only furniture.

A lean man with black hair sits behind the desk. Sweat forms at his hairline. Mills stands before him, the golden handle of his cane gripped tightly in his aged hand.

Two Reapers guard him on each side.

"You didn't tell me you were coming today," the man says, almost in a whisper.

"Are you suggesting I need permission?" Mills' tone demands respect.

"No, not at all, it's just—"

"It's just *what*, Mr. Finch?"

"We aren't quite finished gathering all the data, yet. Just give me and my team a couple more days, and I promise you that it'll be done."

Mills laughs, an unimpressed laugh that sucks the room dry of any hope. "A couple of days? Mr. Finch, I put you in charge of this project to ensure its speed and accuracy. It's been months, and still the Maiden's Touch isn't complete. We only have a couple of more days before it's due for deployment. The genocide *cannot* be delayed."

"Master, I understand, and it *will* be finished. Why are you so worried? The population is calm, You haven't had any Saints patrolling, there isn't a curfew, and not one *single* public execution has occurred in months. For all they know, they're just getting a mandatory shot that will heal their infirmities."

"Jason Pinder is still alive—"

"Jason Pinder hasn't been seen in almost half a year."

"Don't ever interrupt me! I am your God, and you will listen to me!"

Finch tenses. "I'm so sorry, I didn't mean to offend you. The Maiden's Touch will be ready in time. Ahead of schedule, even. I won't let you down, I promise."

"You're right, you won't. . . because I'm not giving you the opportunity." He snaps his fingers.

Both Reapers raise their weapons.

Finch screams out a plea. A handful of bullets penetrate his body. Chunks of flesh, bone, and clothing fly.

Mills scrutinizes the gore now dripping from the bundle of novels and dictionaries. He clasps his other hand over his cane and sighs, "Go inform Mr. Ashford that his new office is ready." He faces the door, an exaggerated frown on his tight face. "Make sure that he knows the drastic consequences heading his way if this weapon is not ready by launch date."

Both Reapers echo out, "Yes, my lord."

"Good." He opens the door. "Just a few more days until our new world begins. You both should feel honored serving me."

They both agree, and the camera cuts back to Cass. "Most of you will die gruesome deaths, and the rest will be sent to a breeding farm and used as reproductive slaves to repopulate the new world. Joseph Mills is a psychopath who's going to kill you all. Your parents, your siblings, your spouses, your children, dead —and if not dead, turned into caged animals who do nothing but provide clueless, innocent children to an evil man who will do nothing but abuse and torture them." Black tears fill Cass's eyes. "My second chance is gone. . . but I guess now isn't the time to think about that. Lazarus has been fighting for a better tomorrow for as long as I can remember. They've fought for your lives, but now, it's time for you to do that yourselves." She pauses. Terror flashes across her face. "Goodbye."

The screen goes black. I grit my teeth.

I'm sorry your second chance ended, Cass.

I turn to the camera placed atop the tripod next to me. There's an HDMI cord hanging from one of its ports. I take it and plug it into the computer, backing out to the main page of the broadcast application.

Instead of selecting the upload option, I click *Livestream*.

More gunshots burst in the distance. This time, it's closer.

Blaine swears from outside the room.

The screen counts down from ten, showing the camera's point of view. I point the lens toward me and step back a foot or two.

Three.

Two.

One.

The livestream starts. I see my pale face, my messy black hair that's turning blond at the roots, my electric blue eyes, and the scar that runs from my left eyebrow down to my cheek.

"A God? Joseph Mills, a withering old fool, is a God?" I glare. "He can torment us, commit mass genocide, and start over, but that doesn't make him omnipotent. It makes him a psychopath who needs to be put down. Lazarus has been working for years to kill this maniac, and now, it's your turn to do something. Don't let him kill off our population, using whoever survives as breeding animals to create an ignorant civilization for his sick use. Take a stand. Help us cut the head off the snake." More gunshots erupt just down the hall. I know I'm running out of time. "Do it for your freedom. For your wife, your husband, your children, and for your lives. Take a stand. Help us hunt down and kill every Saint, Reaper, and official, then, when the structure of this autarchy falls apart, we'll put a bullet in Mills' head. My name is Jason Pinder, and—"

The door behind me is forced open.

I turn just in time to see the immortal Reaper charging at me. Muscle memory kicks in. I dodge his advance, and he crashes into the camera, barreling into a desk.

Chloe rushes in, Blaine following close behind. He aims his pistol at the freak and sends multiple bullets through his chest.

Unfazed, the immortal turns to me. Black blood oozes from his mouth, staining his bared teeth.

My gaze lowers to his waist. He charges once again, and I notice two EMP grenades attached to his belt.

Just like Robyn.

Hell yeah.

I dive out of the way as he nears. He grabs my leg mid-air and hurls me at a wall.

Using words that would make my mother cry, I crash through the plaster and into a wooden beam.

All air escapes from my mouth.

"Jason!" Chloe screams.

The Reaper makes another charge for me, but Chloe lunges onto his back, digging her knife into his throat.

He acts like this is more of an annoyance, keeping his eyes focused on me.

I try to move.

He slams into me, crushing the beam and shoving me further into the wall. He wails his fists down on my face, each strike knocking my vision different colors.

"You-will-not-stop-God!" Every syllable is enunciated.

Chloe wraps her arms around his neck and pulls with all her might, forcing him away. Before he can stumble back too far, I reach for his waist, prying an EMP from his belt. I deploy it.

He throws his head into her nose, grabbing a fistful of blond hair and throwing her to the ground.

Our eyes meet. A smile sweeps across my face, and his veins bulge from his gored neck.

The blast goes off and he collapses to the floor, his body seizing. The familiar black ooze floods from his eyes, ears, mouth, and nose.

I place both hands around the outer edges of the broken wall, pulling myself to my feet. Then, taking my knife out, I straddle the shaking Reaper.

Blaine stumbles closer and helps Chloe to her feet.

"N-N-No—" the Elite stammers, each limb jolting, foam bubbling from his lips.

I pin him down, placing my blade against his throat. "Lights out, piss-face."

Thunder rumbles, and I slice through his flesh, separating his head.

CHAPTER TWENTY-THREE

Saints bludgeoned to death, civilians with their faces blown to bits, cars on fire, blood submerging the streets. The surrounding scenery fills me with both excitement, and angst as a group of rioters charge toward a brigade of soldiers.

We join.

Bullets fly our way. Three men up front are shredded. We make contact.

There's nothing but red as I slash and shoot my way to victory.

Blaine gets tackled to the ground by a Saint. I slice his attacker's throat.

Another solider seizes us from behind. My gun swings around and lodges two bullets in his face.

A civilian at my side eats a shotgun blast.

I get revenge.

"Jason!" Chloe tosses a solider my way.

My foot connects with his kneecap. He collapses, and a bullet drills his brain.

Another Saint charges. I side-step and hurl him at Chloe, who thrusts a blade through his throat.

Gunfire erupts from across the ravaged downtown street.

Dozens of our supports are massacred, their bodies shield us as I grab Chloe and Blaine.

We dive behind a flipped car.

Corpses rain to the asphalt.

Blaine swears. The vehicle gets riddled with bullets. "What the hell do we do now?"

The noise is loud enough to burst my eardrums. "They can't shoot forever."

Strangely, the gunfire ceases. The dreadful sound of marching boots on pavement takes its place. The soldiers move in unison, and the closer they get, the more I'm thrown into overdrive.

Chloe nudges me. "Hurry, we've gotta think. There's got to—"

My soul leaps out of my skin as a horn sounds off. Peeking over our makeshift cover, awe replaces my fear. I behold the aftermath of a semi-truck plowing through the marching squad.

The truck skids to halt, dragging bodies along with it. Its wheels twist limbs and mush heads.

"Well, I guess that works, too," Chloe mumbles.

Both doors to the semi-truck open and two men hop out. They each wear a ski mask I bet they took from a couple of dead Saints.

The driver's eyes light up. There's a rifle in his hands. "Are you him? The one from the broadcast?"

My people skills are kinda off for the night, so I just nod.

His buddy smiles. "Thank you. You gave us that last nudge we needed to stand up and end this."

The gratitude is uncomfortable.

A door opens to the left. I turn to a group of civilians leaving a small store. Behind us, more commotion. Armed insurgents appear from a side street.

Blaine shifts to all those who are unarmed. "Are you guys willing to fight?"

Some of them say yes. He motions them over and points at the weapons gripped by bloody, dead hands. "Pick a gun and start hunting."

They do.

I meet the insurgents behind us. "Where are you all coming from?"

The man standing up front spits. "From the north end of town. The military is held up in few buildings and sending out small groups of soldiers every half hour or so to try and stop us. We put up a good fight, but we're running low on manpower."

The truck driver speaks, "And if you're wondering, me and my buddy are coming from Chinatown. Most of the rioters down there have been killed off, but you could say the same for the Saints."

"Any updates on other cities or states?" Chloe asks abroad.

"From what I've heard, chaos is spreading across the entire nation. I can't tell who's winning, though," an insurgent replies.

I lean up against the flipped car. "It's us, don't worry—"

The top floor of a business complex down the street explodes. The ground beneath us rumbles. Pure adrenaline floods my veins as flames erupt from the building, some of the debris wiping out random vehicles below.

Blaine grabs a rifle off the street, looking my way. "So what now, dudezo?"

I glimpse at the group of insurgents. "You willing to get back into the fight?"

The man upfront nods. "Anything you need us to do, we'll get it done."

"And you two?" I ask the truck drivers.

They affirm.

I step away from the car, motioning the insurgents over. "Get in the storage container on the back of the truck." My eyes shift to the driver. "I want you to drive through the north end. The guys in the back will gun down any soldiers you come across. After you feel it's clear, make your way to the west end, do the same thing, and end your route at Beacon hill."

"What about us?" one of the new recruits ask. He stands next to Blaine.

"I want you and your buddies to patrol the surrounding streets. Rescue any wounded and kill every soldier you see." I finally face the few citizens who don't want to fight. They stand scared, not knowing what to do. "You three. Find a place to hide. Tonight's far from over."

They meekly turn and head back into building they just emerged from.

I pull my backpack off, reaching inside and grabbing two hand radios. I give one to the insurgent's front man, and toss the other to the truck driver. "Switch it to channel eight, that way you'll be able to communicate with each other. I'll be on channel nine if you need me."

"Where are you going?" the driver asks.

"I was thinking me and my partners cou—" Gunfire erupts down another street. My lungs fill, then deflate. "Just go. We'll be in touch."

They nod.

Chloe, Blaine, and I jog to the end of the boulevard. More gunfire echoes off each building and a woman screams.

We run faster.

After turning right at the end of Oliver Street, I stop dead in my tracks.

She stands amid a group of armed Reapers. They're gunning down other insurgents closing in on them, slowly making their way toward a looming, dark structure that stands tall in the murky night sky.

The Sweet Spider. Vice's old hotel.

Chloe's eyes mimic mine, and the months of unspeakable rage built up in her system break free. She screams, *"Robyn!"*

CHAPTER TWENTY-FOUR

Sprinting through the halls of the Sweet Spider, I can't help but think of him. His thick Boston accent, the jet-black suit, and the mask. I'll never forget the mask. My chest is scarred from when he blasted bullet after bullet through me. The force threw me to the ground and left me hysterical, laughing my way into insanity.

Vice. My old puppeteer. He was decapitated on the front lawn of the Estate.

Robyn turns at the end of one of the hallways. Two Reapers stay behind to fight.

An unstoppable force, Chloe tears one of their throats apart with a flying bullet. Sticky red squirts over his partner. Blaine puts him down with another projectile.

His brain spatters across the back wall.

We rush after our prey, each step fueled by revenge.

Raphael.

He chuckled before that hag put a blade in his eye. He was gone quick, but it wasn't pretty.

*Ja-Jason? Eveefing's **black!** Am-Am I **thying?***

"You can't run from this!" I howl as she comes into view.

Chloe fires a bullet. It rips through Robin's shoulder, and she lurches forward, refusing to stop despite black spurting from her.

"You don't know what you're doing!" she yells, fleeing up a flight of stairs.

All her Reapers are dead. She's out of luck. She can only run until she hits an inevitable dead end.

Blaine and I continue to chase. Chloe rushes to an elevator.

I don't question it.

Blaine fires a few rounds. "Where are you going to go, huh!"

She yelps, a bullet puncturing her hamstring. Her veins flow with the Touch, so she's able to keep sprinting.

She's hunted to the very top floor. The second she passes the bathrooms, two metal doors shutter open and Chloe lunges at her. Even after being shot in the back and leg, she dodges out of the way.

She runs into a giant conference room at the end of the hall. The area around me isn't foreign. I remember it all too well.

"God will save me!" Robyn shreds her trench coat and throws it our way. "Just you wait!"

She barges through the doors of the conference room. The adrenaline within me reaches its peak and I rip the EMP grenade from my belt, activating it and hurling it at her.

It goes off and she falls to the floor, smacking her head against the large table placed center of the room. She seizes. Black blood floods through each opening in her face.

We stand over her, our guns pointed at vital areas.

I snarl, "I told you, you can't run from this." My fingers wrap around the trigger.

She seizes a moment longer, gasping for air. "Does this satisfy you? Does seeing God's *bride* defeated like this bring you joy, you filthy parasites?"

"Yes," Chloe mutters.

"I should've killed you the night we first met. You were

helpless tied to that nasty old chair. It would've been so easy, so simple."

"It would've, but you missed your opportunity."

"It was fun torturing and watching you break." Her unnatural eyes meet mine. Robyn's words are chocked out by the black ooze coming from her mouth "She would sob your disgusting name, but you were never there to help. . . poor thing."

The flames in my chest rage. I don't say anything.

"God should have listened to me," she persists. "He's far too guilty of keeping you Lazarus pests imprisoned to show the world you're worthless. Personally, I would have just slaughtered you and that would be the end of it. He likes making a point."

"No," Blaine glares. "He likes being a psychotic freak who wants nothing but worship and attention."

Robyn spits blood at his feet. "Show some respect and bite your filthy tongue."

"Do you really believe that walking corpse is God?" I'm eager to kill her. "He's a psychopath who'll kill you the second you fulfill his needs—not that you'll be able to after we're done here."

"You won't kill me."

Laughter bursts from my mouth. "And what the *hell* makes you say that?"

She slowly grabs the bottom of her black turtleneck and lifts, revealing a swollen stomach. "You may be the devil himself, but even you must have some twisted sense of morality when it comes to the unborn."

"You're pregnant?" Blaine's finger carefully retreats from the trigger.

"With the son of God. He'll be the first of many who will bow down and see our leader for what he truly is. A deity."

"You're so indoctrinated, it's insane." Chloe's shoulders straighten up.

Robyn meets her gaze. "Am I? Am I, really? This world is

polluted with a vile population. A population who's wicked, violent, and defiant. We need a fresh start—"

"Yeah, you're right," I interrupt. "A fresh start without you, or your *God*."

Her stretched grin works hard to cross her face. "Do you miss sweet Raphael?" she chuckles, her teeth smeared in black. "I have pretty good aim, don't I?"

I grab a fist full of her auburn hair and drag her through the exit.

"Let go of me!"

She struggles, but Chloe puts a bullet in her knee.

I pull her to the elevator. "You're going to know true suffering."

Yelping, she desperately claws at my hands. The pain doesn't register. Nothing's going to stop this.

Chloe presses the button that opens the elevator doors. The four of us enter.

Blaine selects the rooftop button. I'm grateful that he's able to read me the way he does.

The doors shut in unison with a chime.

"You can't do this to me!" Robyn struggles some more. "Do you have any idea how important I am to this plan! How much I'm needed?"

"That's exactly why this is happening," Blaine mutters. "So shut the hell up."

We reach our stop, and the doors open. The storm overhead has died down a bit.

I drag her out of the metal compartment, forcing her to the edge of the roof. Below, chaos and bloodshed reign. Gunfights take place in the streets. Corpses litter the city, and numerous buildings surrounding us drown in flames.

"This is what happens when your handler plays God," I say, releasing her hair. "Do you see the bloodbath? The carnage?"

She glares up, snarling, "This is your fault."

My legs move instinctually as she swings a hidden blade my way. I wrap my fingers around her wrist and twist it to the side. Her bone snaps like a twig.

Bellowing out a cry, she swiftly raises her shirt. "*Innocent! You can't! You won't!*"

I lower my gun to her nasty face. "You think I give a damn?"

"Just you wait! This little crusade of yours is going to get you killed! You won't live much longer."

"Funny," I mutter. "Neither will you."

"Idiot! I can't die! It's impossible!"

My foot connects with her face. I back up and look at Chloe. "She's all yours."

Wearing an expression I have never seen before, Chloe steps behind Robyn, squatting next to her broken body. She grabs her by the hair and forces her to sit upright, wrapping her legs around her waist and locking her feet together. A trap she won't escape.

She leans in close. "I'm going make you regret what you did to me."

"Tormenting you was quite the pleasure. I'm still so fond of the taste of your blood."

Chloe takes her knife and slashes it across her torturer's throat. The gash deepens as she saws the blade back and forth. A guttural growl explodes from Chloe's lips. Robyn's arteries, windpipe, and jugular are severed. There's no stopping until her head is dangling by a string of flesh.

We give her a moment.

"Is this really happening?" Blaine steps by my side

"Yeah." I face the city. Several streetlights below have Saints hanging from them. "I'm pretty sure Boston's almost ours."

"It's been a long fight, man."

"Tell me about it."

"I never thought it would go down like this. . . It was almost over for us."

"Yeah. . . You know, sometimes I think there's an actual being in the sky who created us."

"Really?"

"Yeah, and maybe, *just* maybe, he was ready for the suffering to stop, too."

Chloe's sobs gain my attention. She continues to mutilate Robyn's body. I can't decide if I should step in or not.

Blaine puts a hand on my shoulder. "Go to her, man."

I nod, treading over. She stabs, and I kneel, "Hey."

Black splashes against her flushed cheeks. At first, there's no eye contact, but the second there is, she collapses into me. "She— it's just— she really hurt—"

"It's okay. I get it," I soothe.

She cries into my blood-spattered hoodie. Her sentences are never complete, but she talks about the unspeakable things Robyn did. I never wanted to know. Ignorance was welcomed.

The urge to lodge a few bullets into Robyn's body moves me to hurl her head off the building. I need the ammo, so that was the next best thing.

"I'm sorry," I say to Chloe. "I won't let anyone hurt you ever again."

"I know," she whispers.

We embrace.

"You did it. It's over. You can start to heal," I say.

She sighs, "Thanks for sticking by me through it all."

"For you, I'd do anything."

"What happens next?"

"We turn Boston into a sanctuary. We take back the other cities and put an end to this for good."

Blaine steps toward us. "You know people are going to look to you for leadership, right?"

Another explosion rings out a few blocks away. "Yeah. I'm ready."

If you would've asked the me before Lazarus if I thought

something like this was possible, I'd tell you to shut the hell up because the if the wrong ears heard such a thing, we'd all get gunned down.

Chloe wipes her eyes. "And we'll be right there with you."

"Always," Blaine promises.

CHAPTER TWENTY-FIVE

THREE MONTHS LATER

I smooth my thumb across the silver rock with red etched into it. I'm growing sentimental. I carry it wherever I go. Chloe was right when she said it was good luck, because that's all we've really had these past few months.

Well, sort of.

Sebastian Gray, one of my elite scouts, gives me his latest report. His jet-black hair can only cover up so much of the annoyance radiating from his gray eyes. "As we all know, after Boston and the other cities were liberated, Mills was chased into hiding with what remained of his military behind the walls surrounding Seattle. Every time one of our squads get close, they're blown to bits by the miniguns that mount the barriers. We can't send in any aircraft, because they have AA guns, and we know that a vast number of spies and assassins are in our midst."

I sit at the head of a large table inside the Boston State House. The second story assembly room is spacious and empty. It's perfect for our important meetings.

Twenty other leaders from various squads listen intently to Sebastian's frustrations. I'm trying my best to trust each of them, but it's a struggle. Mills wants me dead—and how can I possibly see through the false persona of a spy or assassin? There have only been a handful of them caught, and they're either dead, or being interrogated. With such a heavy population, there's bound to be more.

"Let's also not forget to mention the two hundred innocent lives that were taken in Ohio last week when Mills launched a drone strike." Kendall Hart's brown hair matches her eyes. She's another elite scout. She crosses her arms and adds, "That needs to be our main discussion today. It's been three months and we still haven't been able to get in and take him out. Every second we wait, more innocent people die."

Aaron Knight, a third scout, smooths a hand through his red hair. "I'm with Hart on this. Seattle is the capitol of the nation, so who knows what other weapons he has at his fingertips. We can't afford to wait any longer."

Sebastian sighs, "You two act like we've just been sitting around. What part of *squads being torn apart by miniguns* don't you understand?"

"Calm down, Gray," another scout orders.

Sebastian looks my way. He's hotheaded, like Raph. "Care to share your input?"

My thumb still smooths over the rock. "Sebastian and his teams have put in hundreds of hours trying to breach Seattle. It's an actual miracle he's even alive, so cut him some slack." My eyes find Hart. "I see what you're saying, though. Do you have any ideas?"

Her arms are still folded, "We could tunnel our way into the city."

"Too risky," Sebastian argues. "Not to mention it would take weeks since you would have to start miles away to avoid the guns."

I scrutinize the people around the table. "Does anyone else here know how we can get in and exterminate this wretch of a man... in a timely manner?"

It's silent. I imagine the comedic sound of crickets.

"No one?" My voice echoes around the spacious room.

"You can't. . ." a voice answers.

He's a newer scout. His eyes are wide and his teeth gnash together.

"Excuse me?" I ask.

He jumps up from his seat and onto the table. He stares down with a psychotic look, "You can't kill God, you idiot!"

He draws a gun, but a bullet hits him before he is able to finger the trigger. Two more shots follow, and the assassin collapses to the marbled floor, blood gushing from his exposed skull.

Blaine casually sits next to me with his feet propped up on the table. The barrel of his pistol smokes.

I stand from my chair. A mixture of emotions burst from my chest, "Are you kidding me? It wasn't bad enough that they were posing as civilians, but now as my scouts? Does anyone else in this room want to blow my damn head off? Huh?"

They all stare. Some shocked, some stone cold.

Spit flies from my mouth, "Well, I have a message for all you other bastards. I will murder your God! I will piss on his corpse and there isn't a thing you can do about it!"

I shove the rock in my pocket and storm out of the room.

"Wait," Chloe pleads, but I exit before anyone can say anything else.

Armed guards greet me as I move past them. I head to the first story of the building, then step outside. The setting sun forces me to squint.

I tread down the wavy staircase leading to the sidewalk.

I can't do this anymore.

Even through all the anger and betrayal, there's no ignoring the beautiful scenery as I traverse through the busy streets of downtown Boston. Some of the buildings are disfigured, but that doesn't change the beauty of the fiery leaves dropping from the tall trees or the blazing sky above.

I pass through one of the many street markets spread throughout the city. Many goods are typically free, but some of the bigger and better items are available for barter.

"Care for an apple, Mr. Pinder?" a child asks as I near the end of the market.

Poisoned. Trying to kill you. Keep moving.

I move past him. His smile fades.

They could be anyone, placed anywhere. There's no safety. I'm as good as dead.

Wait, stop. This is what he wants, to drive you mad.

A rugged breath exits my lungs and out my mouth. Battling my fight or flight response, I turn around, "Yeah, actually I would."

The kid's smile returns. He puts the apple in my hands. "My mom and I picked these yesterday! She says we only have about another week until harvesting season is over, so these ones are the bestest."

A chuckle. It's fake. "I bet they are, little dude."

He quickly nods, running back to his mom's stand.

I keep moving and my senses lecture me.

Don't eat it.

Eat it.

He's trying to kill you.

Shut the hell up!

Run.

Am I going crazy?

Danger.

Stop it!

Time loses meaning as my legs move one after the other. Entering a small, grassy park with a playground in the middle, I take a seat on the swing set.

The apple trembles in my grip as tears flow.

I know we've had good luck for the most part, but that doesn't mean I've been able to sleep. I lie every morning when Chloe wakes up. She'll look over and see me awake, and I have to convince her that I've only been up for a couple of minutes, not the whole night.

I'm too scared to close my eyes, because whenever I do, I'm either plagued with nightmares or a debilitating paranoia.

"Why?" I whisper, more tears rolling down my cheeks. It's pathetic. "Why did you put me as your heir?" I gaze up at the now violet sky. "Huh, Raph! Why'd you do it? Did you think it was funny? Some kind of sick joke?"

I throw the apple as hard as I can. It spatters against the playground.

My shoulders shake as I grip the two chains suspending me in the air. I squeeze them until my fingers threaten to bleed. A growl escapes my mouth.

Mills and his military aren't going to stop, not until I'm dead and everyone around me is injected with the Maiden's Touch.

We shut off the city's water a while back so his men couldn't poison us. We have a specific squad that fetches us water from the harbor. They purify it and hand it out all day long.

Obviously, showers aren't a thing, so most of us bathe in the ocean for personal hygiene. I try calming myself with memories of Chloe going to down to the water to bathe and asking me to go with her. She wanted me to be a look out so nobody would see her naked, not that anyone was out and about past midnight.

Still, I felt special.

It was hard to fight the smile that swept across my flushed face as she pulled me into the freezing water with her. She wrapped herself around me.

I hear a twig break. Turning, I see Chloe enter the park.

"There you are," she gasps, wiping sweat from her forehead. "Man, I wish I had longer legs."

"What are you doing here?" I ask.

"Well, geez, I wonder? It's not like you were almost just killed, or anything like that."

"Is now really the time for sarcasm?"

She approaches the swing set. "Sorry, I've been hanging around Blaine too much."

Chloe sits on my lap and hugs me.

"Mills is going to drive me insane," I say.

"No, he's going to *try*, but you aren't going to let him. Blaine and Sebastian already went to go find some answers, so you don't need to worry about it. We're going to get it taken care of."

"It's not just that. It's the drone strike on Ohio, our diminishing resources, the rising stress in the streets. It's been three months, Chloe. *Three*, and we still haven't found a way to breach Seattle and put an end to all this. Last week was Ohio, but what about this week? Or the next? We aren't safe until he and the rest of his followers are dead, and who knows how long it'll be until that's a reality."

She softly pushes away from me. Her green eyes pierce my soul. "You sound so defeated. Are you forgetting who you are or what you've done? He's making you think he's all powerful, but in all actuality, he's hiding. He's scared, hoping and praying you let your guard down, or we surrender."

Through the tears, I chuckle, "Who do you think he prays to? Himself?"

"Probably."

"How are we supposed to win when I can't even trust our scouts anymore?"

"I feel like you can trust Sebastian, Aaron, and Kendall."

"You do?"

"Yeah, they give off good vibes."

"But what if—"

"Trust me. They've been alone with you on multiple occasions and haven't tried to kill you. Not to mention, they've been here since the beginning. I know they aren't shady."

"How do you keep so calm?"

"Because I know everything's going to be okay."

"How could you possibly know that?"

"I just do." She gets off my lap and grasps my hand. "Come on."

I reluctantly stand as she drags me toward the play fort, "I wanna be lazy."

She lets go as we near the stairs and climbs to the top before disappearing.

I stand on the first step, taking a deep breath before chasing after her. At the top. I look around. There's nothing.

"Chloe?" I call out, nearing one of the slides. "Where'd you—"

As I peer down the dark tunnel, she reaches up and grabs the base of my hoodie. We tumble down the slide, and I smack my head against the roof.

"Ow," I groan, suppressing a laugh as we come to a stop. "What are you doing?"

She's lying on top of me. Her nose touches mine. "I've got a little something to tell you."

"What? That all the trauma we've been through has turned you into a vegetarian?"

"What? No—"

"I've seen you curl your nose whenever Blaine and I cook dinner. Either our burgers suck, or—"

"I'm pregnant."

Pregnant?

That word shoves anxiety down my throat. She's joking. "When did you become a comedian?"

She smiles. "I'm not kidding. I went to the hospital earlier today to see one of the doctors about my nausea, and they gave me a pregnancy test. It came back positive."

I stare at her for an eternity. A feeling I've never felt before blooms within me, "Wait. . . so you're telling me that we're going to be. . . parents?"

The euphoric feeling intertwines fear and love and throws it in a blender. I fight the urge to vomit—sort of in a good way, sort of in a bad way.

"Calm down there, bucko." She kisses me. "You look like you're gonna faint."

"You're really not kidding, are you?"

"If I was, that'd be pretty messed up."

My stomach churns. I abruptly move her out of the way, lunging from the slide and spewing my guts all over the bark.

"Shouldn't I be the one doing that?" she asks.

Despite the smile on her pretty face, tears trickle down her cheeks.

Soon enough, I mirror her emotional display.

"How far along are you?" My posture gently straightens.

"I think like six weeks, they said."

We both laugh a bit. Some of it is to get the fear out of our system. Then, the excitement.

We embrace. I hold her as tight as I can. Her tears soak my hoodie.

"Blaine's gonna kill us," she jokes.

"I owe him five bucks."

"He's so weird."

"But that's why we love him."

"That's true."

I sniffle, then ask, "How are we going to raise in kid in a world like this?"

"We can't. That's why you can't give up. We need to put an end to this madness so we can create a new normal together."

"Mills won't be breathing for much longer. I'll make sure of that."

"I know you will."

"I love you."

"I love you, too. Always."

The radio attached to my belt chirps.

"You there, dude?" Blaine's voice pours through.

Chloe and I part. Grabbing the device, I bring it up to my mouth. "Yeah, I'm here. What's up?"

"Sebastian and I are at Warehouse A. Think you can meet us here?"

"Is it important? I'm kind of in the middle of something."

"Well, what do you classify as important?"

"Anything in relation to killing Mills."

"Then you might wanna hurry. That one spy we took prisoner last week has finally woken up from his mini-coma and boy does he *love* pissing me off."

My eyes widen. "Is he talking?"

"Nope, that's the problem, but we're sure you could get him to open his pretty little mouth." In the background, Sebastian shouts obscenities. Blaine clears his throat. "So, see you soon?"

"I'll be there in fifteen."

"Sounds good."

The channel goes dead.

Chloe shoots me a half smile. "Go do what you gotta do."

"I will."

She gives me another hug. "We've got this, okay?"

"I know we do." I rub my palm across her back.

She whispers, "I know this is kind of a side note, but I'm happy your hair is back to normal."

"Oh, what, you didn't like it when it was black?"

"You looked too edgy."

I roll my eyes, giving her a kiss. "Meet me back at the State House in a bit?"

"Yes, sir."

"And you'll be safe?"

"Always am."

"Good."

We go separate ways, and I'm given another reason to live. I smile at the thought of a little us, a kid who can grow up in a peaceful world.

The possibility closes up some open wounds. I'm ready to do whatever it takes.

CHAPTER TWENTY-SIX

I pound my fist against the door of Warehouse A.
 I'm weightless.
One of the two double doors slide open, revealing Blaine.
"Took you long enough," he jokes. There's blood sprinkled across his pale face.
"Better late than never, yeah?"
"Yeah."
He opens the door a bit more and I step inside the spacious building illuminated by artificial lights above. We don't store anything here. There's only a single metal chair placed in the center of the large room. A bloodied, almost naked man is handcuffed to it.
He's young. Maybe a few years older than me.
Sebastian is beating his face in. His knuckles are stained.
"So, this is the lucky guy, huh?" I ask. Sebastian glances back.
"Indeed he is." Stepping aside, he motions me over. "He's all yours, bossman."
The spy shifts in his chair as I approach. His right eye is purple, his lip is busted, and his wrists are swollen from the restraints.

"You're the one who was taking videos of our meetings and sending them back to Seattle, right?" I ask despite knowing the answer. "Did you really think we wouldn't notice?"

He scowls, "You won't win this."

"And you think you will?"

"We have immortality."

"Do you have any idea know how many *immortals* I've killed?"

He doesn't say anything. Instead, he spits blood at my feet.

"Tough guy, yeah? How many more of you are there?"

"Sorry, I don't know how to count."

I skid my knuckles across his face. "Do you really want to be a smartass?"

He flashes a bloody grin. "Yeah."

I hit him again, and this time I don't stop until his face is almost unrecognizable.

Blaine nears me with a wicked smile. "I think we need to amp things up, Jay."

I agree, pulling my gun out and aiming it at the spy. "How many more of you are there?"

"You won't kill me, not as long as I have the information you want."

I blast one of his kneecaps apart. He screams, the sound piercing the air as blood pours from his exposed flesh.

I aim at the other. "How many more are there? I want an exact number, and where to find them."

He keeps screaming. I grit my teeth, blasting the other apart. "How many?"

"Too many!" His shrills echo against the concrete walls. He thrashes in the chair so violently that it threatens to break. "Too many to count, you parasite!"

I swipe my gun across his face. "Where?"

"You can't kill God! He will take this nation back and continue his work, and there isn't a thing you can do about it!"

Suddenly his head explodes. Chunks of skull and brain shower me as the screaming abruptly stops.

The warehouse drowns in silence.

Sebastian speaks first, "What the. . .?"

A voice projects through the spy's open neck. "Don't you just adore the smell of gore?"

Mills.

Blaine tilts his head. "Wait, is that *him*?"

"I love hearing you so shocked, Mr. West. It's a beautiful thing." His voice is the epitome of arrogance. "Why don't you boys go look at the nearest screen?"

My blood runs cold. The three of us hurry to the entrance. I slide one of the doors open.

A large billboard flickers to life, illuminating the darkened sky. It shows a busy downtown market where the men are trading, the women are chatting, and the children are playing.

Sebastian raises an eyebrow. "Where is that?"

In the night sky above the market, a plane comes into view. It drops napalm over the civilians, the scene bursting into flames. The footage soon stops and switches to Mills. He's sitting in the back of a vehicle.

"I'm taking my nation back." There's a smile on his face. "Last week, it was Ohio, but today, New York. I truthfully don't care if you surrender or not, because regardless, I'm wiping your cities clean and injecting anyone remaining with the Touch." His eyes widen with glee. "And if you still aren't frightened, just know that my spies and assassins fill your ranks. They could be your next-door neighbors, your friends down the street, or even some of the top dogs in charge of your new order. You're all going to die, and I relish that."

He bursts into a fit of laughter. The stream ends.

Blaine, Sebastian, and I exchange looks. Without a word, we run to our car, panic pulsing through our frantic minds.

Sebastian gets behind the wheel and starts the engine. He takes us into the city.

Hell has broken loose.

All around me, people are going crazy. On one side of the street, a group of civilians are beating a man to death with pipes and bats. On the other, a few kids are shoving another down to the street and stomping him.

"What's wrong with them?" Blaine asks. Sebastian turns right at an intersection.

"They're horrified." I don't know what to feel. Is it anger? Fear?

Sebastian slams on the brakes. The road ahead is blocked by more rioting.

"Back up," Blaine orders, but a woman screams for help.

I search for the source and see a group of men attacking a young girl. One of them pulls away at her shirt, and another goes for her jeans.

Moving without thought, I swing the door open, rushing from the car. "Get the hell off her!"

They look but aren't dissuaded.

"Back off!" one of them yells.

I throw him to the ground, stamping his face before rushing his buddy. He swipes my jaw.

I headbutt him.

He tries to kick my shin.

I shoot him in the head.

The rest of them yelp, scrambling to their feet and scattering.

The girl on the ground hurries to her feet, tears streaking down her cheeks, "Thank you."

"Hurry, you gotta get out of here."

"I don't know where my boyfriend is. Where should I go?"

"Anywhere but here," Blaine shouts from the car. "Now come on, Jason. We've gotta go."

I pat her on the shoulder. "Get inside. This will be over in just a few minutes."

She thanks me a final time before running away. I get back in the car.

"Nice hero-boner," Blaine remarks. I shut the door.

"Not now." My thoughts veer to Chloe. I don't know where she is. I've gotta stop this. "Sebastian, get us to the state house."

"Working on it," he says, backing up and taking a left at the intersection.

As we speed through the chaos, my mind won't let me think of anything else. What if that girl on the street was her? Could the same thing be happening to her, right now?

No. She'd kill anyone who got that close. She's going to be okay.

Sebastian swears as a dude is hurled into the street by the mob. His body crashes into the hood of our car and is mangled by our speed.

I grip the grab handle mounted to the ceiling.

It's going to be a long night.

CHAPTER TWENTY-SEVEN

Rushing to the second story of the state house, my mind is still stuck on Chloe. I try to push the thought of her being attacked aside and focus on the task at hand, but it's almost impossible.

"We're almost there." Blaine brings up the rear as we run up the stairs.

Reaching the top, I race to the door that leads to the balcony. There's such little time to catch my breath. The cool November breeze blows my hair.

Blaine hands me a wireless microphone. "Here."

"You're sure it's connected?" I ask, sweat pouring down my frame.

"Positive."

Sebastian appears behind us.

There's too many jumbled thoughts in my head I have to organize. With one last deep breath, I turn the mic on and raise it to my lips. "Everybody needs to calm down. Stop the anarchy, the killing, the rioting, and listen." My voice reverberates throughout Boston due to speakers that are placed around the city. "Mills is a monster who thrives on chaos. He wants you to snap, to feel helpless, to turn on each other, but you can't. We need every single person listening to band together and keep this city running, so *please* stop." The city seems to stand still. "He mentions spies and assassins, but we've already known this. We've captured over a dozen of these bastards. We will stop them. You need to stop dragging your friends, your neighbors, or your enemies through the street in the name of justice, because the next one of you who harms another will be executed. We are better than this."

"Amen," Sebastian mutters.

"We're supposed to be a unified community with the pursuit of independence and happiness." My voice fills with the hope for my own future. "I'm sending my scouts out, and anyone who is still rioting will be arrested; and to reiterate, anyone who harms another human being who isn't a *confirmed* Saint or Reaper, will be put to death. Go inside, calm your families down, and remember that our main purpose is defeating Joseph Mills and rebirthing this nation for a better tomorrow."

I cut the mic.

Blaine pulls his radio from his belt and raises it. "Attention all scouts, this is Blaine, do you copy?"

A storm of affirmatives burst through the receiver.

"Good. I need each of you and your squads to patrol the streets. Like Jason said, anyone who's caught rioting is to be arrested."

"And kill those who are harming others?" a random scout inquires.

"Within reason. Try to arrest them too so we can run a fair trial and see if their actions were justified or not. We don't want to put people down like dogs. We aren't Mills."

"Yes, sir."

I pick my radio up as well. "Kendall and Aaron. Get to the meeting room, asap."

The two of them respond, "Copy."

The door to the balcony swings open. It's Chloe. She's sprinkled in blood with a blade gripped in her hand and a scowl on her face. "We're not waiting another second to put that freak down."

CHAPTER TWENTY-EIGHT

Sitting around the large table in the meeting room, Chloe, Blaine, Sebastian, Aaron, Kendall, and I exchange stares. The giant clock mounted on the back wall ticks with every passing second.

"We're running out of time." Chloe is the first to speak. "After Mills' strike on New York, I wouldn't be surprised if we're next."

"I agree." Sebastian sits up in his chair. "His spies are deactivating the AA guns each city has since both Ohio and New York had them. I think we need to send a squad over to the base at the edge of town and make sure ours are online."

I smooth my fingers over the rock Chloe gave me. "Chloe and I can do that after this meeting."

"What exactly are you hoping to get out of this, sir?" Aaron asks. His brown eyes rest on me.

I'm sick of this. I'm sick of the wait. "We need a way to kill Mills—not tomorrow, not next week. Tonight. He needs to be gone by sunrise."

Kendall's eyes widen, "*Sunrise?* There's no way."

"That's bull," Blaine chimes. "There's a way to do everything."

The room goes quiet. Aaron eventually says, "There's one way we could actually accomplish this."

"Which is?" I inquire.

"It's practically calculated suicide, but there's no doubt in my mind that it would work. We take one of the jets that have an auto pilot feature and send it to Seattle. The speed of the jet along with its AA countermeasures would give us a window where we could jump from the aircraft and parachute into the city. From there, we fight our way to the Estate and assassinate Mills."

"That's actually genius," Kendall awes.

"I'm down," Sebastian says.

They look at the rest of us for feedback. Blaine is the first to speak out.

"I don't know about the whole *calculated suicide* part, dudezo. Could you elaborate?" he asks.

Aaron appears cold. "After we kill Mills, escape would most likely be impossible. Assuming his whole military is stationed within those walls, and there only being six of us, I can't see a way we'd make it out alive."

"Couldn't we arrange an evac?" Sebastian asks. Some of the enthusiasm drains from his face.

"That would have to be by helicopter, so unless you enjoy watching our people die, I'd say no because of Seattle's numerous anti-aircraft measures."

"Couldn't we just disable them after Mills' dead?" Blaine raises an eyebrow.

"I mean, we technically could, but fighting our way over there would be equally as dangerous."

"I like that better than calculated suicide, though," Kendall remarks.

"Same," Chloe agrees.

Aaron sighs, "It's still suicide, but if you all feel more comfortable calling for an evac and attempting to disable the guns, then we can do that."

Everyone nods, except for me.

They eventually all wait for my answer. My lungs fill. "I like where this is going, but—"

"But what?" Aaron asks.

"I feel like we'd be better off having more people tag along. With only six of us, we'd get overpowered within minutes."

Sebastian fiddles with his handgun. "Are you suggesting we bring the other scouts?"

"It doesn't necessarily have to be the scouts, we just need bodies. I know that sounds horrible, but the more men we have, the better the chances. They don't even have to be at our skill level."

"So, you want them more as a distraction?" Kendall asks.

I exhale, putting my rock back in my pocket, "I'm not going to pretend to be all selfless and honorable with you, so yes. I want men and women who are willing to die that will distract the military long enough for us to get inside the Estate and put an end to this all."

"They'll be slaughtered," Aaron avows. "Especially if they aren't other scouts."

"I'm aware of that," I mutter.

"I know killing the entirety of his military with groundwork isn't realistic," Sebastian starts. "So, after we're gone, I think we should carpet bomb the city. The guns will already be disabled, and there's no way they'll be able to evacuate in such a short amount of time."

"I was just about to suggest something like that," Blaine says.

"Good idea." Aaron looks at me for an affirmation. "Are you okay with this plan, sir?"

It sounds plausible. It's definitely better than anything I would've come up with. I'm about to say yes, but my mind thinks of Chloe and her pregnancy. We're going to be parents.

"I like it." My next words need to be picked very carefully. I turn to Chloe. "But you aren't coming."

"Wait, what?" Her excitement drops. "Why?"

"You know why."

"You can't just tell me to stay here. I'm a part of this, too."

"Chloe."

"Jason."

The rest of the room stares at us. Blaine asks, "Um. . . why wouldn't she be able to come?"

I'm flustered. "She's pregnant."

Her eyes widen. "Way to tell everyone."

Blaine's expression is overwhelmed by shock, but he slowly grins. "You owe me five bucks."

"Shut up," Chloe and I order.

She and I continue our argument. The others grow visibly uncomfortable.

Kendall and Sebastian stand from their seats.

"We're gonna fetch everyone's gear." Kendall quicky leaves, followed by Sebastian.

Blaine and Aaron are right behind them, informing us that they're going to go prep the jets and find volunteers to essentially be massacred.

It's just us now.

Tears form in Chloe's eyes. "You didn't have to tell everyone."

"I wanted to be transparent."

"This is an us thing, not a them thing."

"I'm sorry."

"You can't possibly believe that I'm just going to sit back and let you go without me."

"I can, because that's exactly what you're going to do."

"You don't get to order that."

"But I do."

"Can you drop the brooding leader persona and actually talk to me?"

"I am talking to you."

"But you aren't. You're giving orders, not communicating your feelings."

"We don't have time for that. Not when there's unrest in the streets, spies and assassins trying to kill us, and an imminent threat of being bombed. We're out of options, okay? And—"

"And what?"

"And I wouldn't be able to live if anything happened to you."

"But you can go and die? Show everyone that you're the hero, again?"

"That's not what this is. Why would you even say that?"

"The only thing I'm taking away from our conversation is you can't live without me, but I'm magically supposed to deal with your death if it happens. What about my feelings, Jason? Have you ever considered that I love you just as much as you love me? That I would be just as broken if anything bad happened to you?"

"Chloe—"

"No. This is exactly what got Raphael killed. You're being reckless."

"What do you expect me to do?"

"Not go. If I'm not going, then neither are you."

"Mills is mine. If anyone is going to kill that bastard, it's going to be me."

"Will you stop with this revenge crap? Mills has to die, I agree, but you don't have to be the one who does it. There's more to life than killing those who wronged you, especially when it puts yourself in danger—"

"That's bold coming from you."

"I'm not saying I don't do the same thing, but all of that was before you knocked me up."

"You don't have to say it like that."

She cries harder, and I can't hold back my own tears.

"Can't you see where I'm coming from?" she asks. "We have a little us to take care of. If you go and get yourself killed, then I have to do it alone, and that isn't something I can do."

A buildup of emotion rises into my throat. "Then why didn't you just leave with me all those months back? Why didn't you just swallow your lust for killing Robyn and leave?"

"You know I had to. I'm sorry."

"I just wanted to run away and hide from all this. I know that's a bitch move, but it's all I really wanted. I wanted us to be safe, to be able to start a family somewhere where the freaking president couldn't find and execute us. Do you know why? Because I'm selfish. I'm a selfish prick who only cares about us. I don't care about the little kids down at the markets, or the bread lady down the street. If they died, it wouldn't mean a thing to me."

"That's not true—"Chloe interjects.

"It is. I only care about you. You're my number one focus. Everything I do, I do it for you."

Her green eyes bore a hole into my soul. Tears freely fall from her eyes. "Then stay here. Please don't go."

I sniffle, biting the inside of my cheek. I think about Mills. About all the horrible things he's done to me, and the people in my life. My shoulders bare the pain, suffering, rage, and endless sorrow he's brought upon me.

Then I think about Chloe and how happy she makes me. I ponder all the moments we've shared, both special and traumatic. She's been there through it all, holding my hand along the way. She's seen me cry, laugh, yell, and kill. She's seen through me, and despite all the bad, still loves me.

And for that, I choose her.

"Okay," I mutter. "I won't go."

Her lower lip trembles. "Do you mean it?"

"Killing him isn't worth my life. I know the others will do fine without me."

She hugs me. "Thank you."

We talk for a while, mostly to calm each other down. We discuss where we want to live after this is all done, and what we want to name our kid depending on the gender.

She picks the name *Evie* if it's a girl. A tribute to her dead sister I haven't heard much about.

On the other hand, if it's a boy, I pick the name *Valentine*.

"Just like our fake last name in Cheshire?" she asks.

"Yeah, I like it a lot, actually. We could call him Val for short."

"That's kinda cute."

The radio attached to my belt squawks. Heavy metal blares in my ears.

Chloe winces at the sudden sound.

"They're everywhere! Holy shi—"

Abrupt gunfire masks the music. The channel goes dead.

Silence encases the room. We exchange looks.

"What was that?" she asks.

My mind searches for an explanation, but in the distance I hear something. At first, it's almost unrecognizable, but the closer it gets, the more audible the sound becomes. It's the same heavy music that was just playing through my radio. It gets louder, and louder, a gritty riff booming through the city.

I get up from the table, grabbing Chloe by the hand and rushing out of the room and into the crowded second story.

Multiple guards are pushing past each other to get to the balcony. I'm more bewildered. They're talking over one another, so when my radio goes off again, I'm unable to make out a single thing that's being said.

We shove past them, ordering everyone away from the balcony. They disperse, and we step out onto the terrace.

My jaw drops and Chloe swears under her breath.

A dark ocean of Saints and Reapers march through the streets of Boston, gunning down fleeing citizens as they slowly approach the State House.

CHAPTER TWENTY-NINE

Heavy metal blasts in my ears as I behold the chaos. Dozens of helicopters fly through the air, massacring crowds of innocent people as they run away in terror.

The music gets louder by the second. It prevents me from thinking properly. The thrashing guitars are accompanied by screaming vocals.

It feels like an attempt to disorient the people. It triggers a fight response in me.

My radio goes off again. I bring it to my ear.

"Jason! Jason this is Kendall! The military is sieging the city. I repeat, the military is sieging the city! They've set up checkpoints all over Boston! I think they're heading straight for you!"

Gunfire bursts from the radio.

"Get your head down!" she yells. The channel goes dead.

Different parts of my body twitch. Too many thoughts. Too many emotions.

Twitch.

Twitch.

Twitch.

Chloe grabs my arm and says something, but I can't hear her. I try to ask her to repeat herself when a helicopter lowers next to the balcony. The noise of its blades accompanied by the music is deafening.

Our eyes squint at a blinding light shining down on us.

The miniguns mounted to its belly spin. I tackle Chloe inside as blazing bullets obliterate the area around us. I throw myself on top of her, and the guards surrounding us are torn to pieces. Chunks of flesh and bones shower the walls and carpet.

My ears ring as their corpses rain. My heart beats out of my chest.

Another few seconds of gunfire, then it stops. The helicopter flies away, and we're left amid the massacre.

I slowly prop myself up, glancing around at the carnage.

The guard collapsed nearest to us stares into nothing. The lower half of his body is stripped of flesh and muscle. "S-sir. . ."

My eyes widen. I reach for my gun and pull the trigger, putting him out of his misery.

The smell of gore and piss hits me like a truck. Before Chloe can ask if I'm okay, I roll off her and puke all over the tattered shoes of another mutilated body.

She cautiously gets to her feet, peering through the opened balcony entrance. "It's gone, but the Saints are getting closer."

I spit, my stomach empty. "Are you hurt?"

"No, what about you?"

"I'll live."

I get to my feet, stepping over each corpse on the way to the staircase.

"Where are you going?" She follows.

"Do you remember when we first took Boston over, and we decided that this would be our outpost?"

"Yeah?"

"Do you remember what we found in the basement our first day?"

"Oh, yeah. Good idea."

We hurry down to the first floor, but what comes into sight leaves my eyebrow raised.

"What the hell. . .?" Chloe mutters. Her eyes fall upon dozens of dead guards.

The front entrance is sealed tight with a barricade around it, so there hasn't been a breach.

Or has there?

I approach the fallen soldiers, noticing that their throats have been sliced open.

Then it dons on me.

"Chloe, look out!"

She turns just in time to see an assassin lunge at her.

One of the *dead guards* jumps up and attacks me.

I dodge his swinging blade before shooting him in the stomach. It doesn't stop him.

He grabs my collar and pulls me in close before pushing away.

I lose my balance.

He grabs my leg and forces it between his thighs. I try to react, but he turns sideways and falls to the ground, taking me with him. He immediately throws himself on top of me, but my lessons in combat overtake my senses, and I thrust my hips.

Stumbling, he's desperate to regain dominance.

I grab a hold of his sleeve and yank him to the side, shifting the balance and getting on top. He yelps as I kneel on his thigh, not allowing a second pass. My gun is pulled and I hurl a bullet through his sweaty forehead.

Chloe struggles with her assailant.

He pins her up against a wall, his blade wrestling toward her throat.

I scramble to my feet and dash.

The assassin feels my approaching steps and throws her at me.

I stumble back as our bodies collide.

The attacker charges. He slices my forearm.

Chloe crashes an elbow against his jaw. This fazes him. We both hammer our fists into his face, knocking him to the ground.

"Wait—" he pleads, but Chloe takes her own gun and fires twice.

Our chests move up and down.

"Do you think there's any more of them?" she asks.

"Knowing our luck? Probably."

My arm catches her sight. Sticky red drips from the open wound. "That's deep."

"I'll be okay. We've gotta get going."

She takes her hoodie off, revealing a black tank top.

"What are you doing?" I ask.

"You're not going to be much help if you pass out from blood loss." She wraps the clothing around my arm and ties it in a knot. "There. Now we can go."

High alert. We head for the basement stairs, anticipating another attack. There's a keypad at the door. She punches in the code, allowing us to descend into the depths of the State House.

"What's the plan once we hit the other side?" she wonders aloud.

"I don't know." The music outside is still audible. "Any ideas?"

"I'm sure everyone's either dead or dying as we speak, so I don't know, either."

Her words defeat me, but I know they're true. Just hours ago, we were at the playground, the city around us calm and peaceful. Now? Well now it's a warzone and everyone we know is probably full of bloody holes.

I should have caught on. During his broadcast, he was in the back of a car. My mind was just too jumbled to connect the pieces. Now we're under siege. I'm an idiot.

We reach the bottom of the steps, walking down a hallway with doors on either side.

My mind wanders to Blaine. I reach for my radio. "Blaine? Blaine, you there?"

The channel crackles to life, but nothing replies except static. I should've known the reception down here would be utter crap.

Chloe looks back at the stairs. "We've gotta go back."

"We can't."

"But he's family."

"The Saints were headed straight for us. I wouldn't be surprised if they're already up at the barricade trying to break through. We have to keep going."

"But what about—"

"We'll figure it out once we get to the other side. He's smart, way smarter than any lousy Saint. He'll be okay."

"Promise?"

"Yes, I promise."

We keep moving, eventually making it to a large metal padlocked door.

She stares. "I don't remember there being a lock."

"Me neither."

She abruptly shoots it off the door. My soul threatens to leap from my body.

"Hey," I object.

"Did you have a better idea?"

"No."

"Exactly. Come on."

She opens the door, and we enter a tunnel.

CHAPTER THIRTY

The constant crackles emitting from my radio fill the silence. Since we're underground, there's never any voices, just an irritating static.

It's dark, cold, and damp. However, there's still a sense of safety that above ground didn't hold. As we traverse our way through the passage, Chloe holds my hand. Her grip gets weaker by the minute.

My tone is soft. "Do you need me to slow down?"

"No, no you're good, it's just—"

"You're pregnant?"

She chuckles regardless of tonight. "Yeah. That."

I smile. It quickly fades. We're under attack and the chances of us living are little to none.

I bet Mills is euphoric right now. I can just picture him laughing with triumph, telling all his followers that *God can't fail*.

My left eye twitches. "I hate this."

"I do, too."

"How didn't I know? If they traveled here, then why haven't our coms been blowing up with scouts telling us that the other states are under siege?"

"If the spies were able to deactivate the AA guns, then they were probably able to disable communications outside of Boston, too."

Her words cause my head to spin.

I wasn't able to reach the head scout of Pennsylvania the other day.

Now that I think about it, I haven't been able to reach anyone that isn't here in the city.

"You're right. . ."

"Are we all that's left?"

"I. . . I don't know. Even if we are, it doesn't matter. We're going to make it through this."

My knuckles beg to be thrown against the cement walls.

You're so stupid! How could you let this happen?

Some time passes before we reach the end of the tunnel. A ladder waits against the back wall, leading above ground.

I go first.

There could be a squad of Saints waiting at the top to kill whoever shows their sorry face. If that's the case, it needs to be me, not Chloe.

I push the latch away.

No one.

All that waits is a dark, sandy beach. The waves crash against the shore, oblivious to the slaughter taking place.

There's no more music blaring. The city and everything around it sounds silent.

I get up and turn, saying, "We're clear."

She climbs to the surface. "I've never been here before."

"To Carson Beach?"

"Yeah. Swimming was never my thing, but who knew it would be so pretty?"

The moon reflects off the water. My eyes eventually rest on a fishing boat bobbing near the shore. It gives me an idea.

"We could just leave. . ."

Gunshots sound off in the distance. Our eyes meet. "Where would we go?"

"Novia Scotia. We could be there by morning if we take that boat."

She eyes it, her expression swirling with temptation. "But what about. . .?" Tears drip down her cheeks. She plants her face against my chest. "I want to say yes."

"Then do it."

"But what about everyone else?"

More gunfire erupts.

Blaine. He's still trapped somewhere in the city.

He could be dead.

Or alive.

I'll never know if we leave.

My throat tightens. "We have a family, Chloe."

She tries to speak several times but fails. Eventually, her lungs deflate. "You're right. . ."

"Are you sure?"

"Yeah. Going back when we don't even know who's alive isn't worth the possibility of losing you."

Tears roll down my cheeks. I grab her hand and lead her to the shore. "I'm sure there's a bunch of cabins over there. We could find one that's big enough for the three of us and start over."

"I like that. It's cute."

I want to keep talking. It eases my filthy conscience. We're leaving everyone behind. What kind of leader disappears when his people are getting slaughtered?

What kind of leader abandons his best friend?

His best friend who has done nothing but support him?

A small wave crashes against our feet. My radio goes off.

"Jason." Blaine's voice pours through. "Jason, I don't know if you're dead or not, but I'm pinned down at the hospital." Gunshots burst through the speaker. He swears, his voice cracking. "Damn it! I just wanted to say thank you for giving me a second chance and believing in me. I love you, man." More shots are fired. Then, "Aaron! Motherfu—"

The channel goes dead.

No.

No, no, no.

I didn't want to know. I could have pretended he was gone.

This forces an ultimatum.

Leave Boston or save Blaine.

In the last two years, I've had my life saved repeatedly by somebody else. I think back to Seattle, and how we were pinned down by Saints. Chloe had died, and same with Blaine. I was on my way out too when Tommy and Marcy killed our attackers and injected us with Rebirth in front of that unfinished hotel.

I remember my time trapped inside the Estate. Dante kept me alive, informing me on what was to come. I'll never forget slitting Mills' throat, and Tommy bursting through that window to fight off those Reapers.

Saving us had its toll, though. He died in my arms later that night.

"It's your choice." Chloe dispels my thoughts.

I jitter, "We can't— let's just— ah! I don't know. I don't know what to do. I have—"

"What would he do in your shoes?"

There's no wondering. "He'd come running."

"Gun and vodka in hand."

"I'm scared."

She holds me tight. "I know. Me too."

I try convincing myself that this is what he'd want. That he'd want me to run far away from here and live my life, but it doesn't work. There's no easing the guilt.

He's fighting for his life. He doesn't want it to end like this. He wants to get married and have a family.

I clench my jaw. "Just wait here. The three of us can leave together. Just give me an hour"

She doesn't argue, just nods. Her cheeks are flushed.

I place a hand on her stomach, our eyes meeting. "I'll be okay, I promise."

"You better."

We kiss goodbye, and I turn away.

Bringing the radio up to my mouth, I stare at the starry-night sky.

I breathe.

Breathe some more.

Then I ask, "Which hospital?"

CHAPTER THIRTY-ONE

My knife sinks deep into the throat of a Saint. Fear shines out from his eyes. I relish it, ripping the blade from his body and jabbing it through his iris.

One of his partners tries to shoot me.

I'm quicker, shooting a bullet through his skull.

An all-out brawl ensues.

A third Saint thrusts a knife my way.

I dodge.

A fourth slams his knuckles against my face.

I stab him in the thigh.

The third thrusts again.

I drop to the ground. He accidently stabs his wounded partner in the chest.

My gun swings and shoots two holes through him. I scoot back, finishing the wounded one off.

A fifth one appears suddenly and kicks me in the ribs, then twice more.

I try to put a bullet in him, but a sixth also shows up and knocks the gun loose from my hand. He lifts me by my hair and lets his buddy get a few punches in.

Crimson spills from my mouth. Chloe's face is framed in my mind. With a sudden burst of adrenaline, I take my knife and skewer the man in front of me. The tip of the blade exits the back of his throat.

He drops like a fly.

His partner lets go of me.

I turn just in time for him to reach for his gun. I lunge forward, stabbing him in his unprotected hip. I reel back and stab again. My face is twisted with rage as I reach up and slash his throat.

He gurgles, dropping to his knees.

I spit on his soon-to-be corpse, stepping over him and grabbing my gun off the sidewalk. Looking up, I see the hospital that Blaine is trapped in. The glass entrance is shattered, and the inside is thrashed.

I have to step over multiple dead bodies, each belonging to my ranks.

Come on, Blaine. Don't let this be for nothing.

A woman screams from one of the halls

It forces me into action.

A Saint pins a nurse up against a wall. He has a gun to her head, laughing. She claws his hand away.

"There's something about a pretty little lady crying that gets me goin—"

My knife enters his temple. He falls to the ground, releasing the nurse from his nasty grip.

"Thank you!" She hugs me. "If you hadn't shown right then, he would've— he would've—"

"You're safe now, it's okay."

"Thank you so much!"

"Have you seen my bodyguard? He's a super pale dude with sunglasses. I need to find him, and he said he was here."

"Y-yeah. He was trying to defend the lobby but was pushed back to the second floor."

"You've gotta hide."

"Where should I go?

"Any room with a lock. You'll be safe there for now."

"Okay. Please be careful. We need you."

"Don't worry about me. Focus on yourself, and you'll make it through tonight."

She runs away. I jog to the staircase, making my way to the top. There's a commotion ahead.

It sounds like a door is being pounded.

Bingo.

I approach the noise, silencing my footsteps. Nearing the end of a hall, I peer around the corner. There's a group of Saints doing exactly what I thought, banging their fists on a door.

"Crap's solid," one of them mutters.

"Yeah, and one of them is already hit. Should we just go?"

I look at the floor. A Lazarus scout lies dead at my feet. Half of his face is missing, but an automatic rifle is limply held in his hands.

I holster my pistol and pick up the new weapon, checking its magazine for ammo. *I'm in luck.* It's full, and without wasting another second, I step out and spray lead into all of them. Blood splashes against the white walls as they drop. Some still struggle for breath, so I jet them a few more times, tossing the gun to the floor.

I yell through the dense wooden door, "Blaine? It's me."

A few moments go by, but the knob eventually twists, and the door opens.

Blaine is kneeling next to Aaron, who's on the ground with his intestines hanging out.

The dying scout looks up, his brown eyes fading. He tries to move his lips but doesn't have the strength.

"I'm out of ammo," Blaine's voice creaks. "You got this one?"

I'm heavy as I take my gun and aim it at Aaron. "You did good. Thank you."

Blaine swallows and looks away.

I pull the trigger.

"They came out of nowhere," he mutters. "We were walking through the streets when that freaking death metal started blasting. Next thing I know, shots were being fired from all around and we hurried inside this place. We kept the lobby protected for almost an hour, but they overwhelmed us, and we got chased up here."

My hand reaches out. "Boston's lost. There's hardly any of us left but a whole bunch of them still standing. Luckily for us, not too many soldiers are roaming the streets anymore. From what I can tell, most of them are occupying some of the bigger buildings while they wait for their orders."

"So, what about us? What are we going to do?" He takes my hand.

"Chloe has a boat waiting for us over at Carson Beach. We're getting the hell out of here."

My words boost his morale. "Wait, are you for real? We've got a way out?"

"Yeah, but we need to hurry. I'm worried that the Saints, or even worse, the helicopters, are going to check the beaches next."

"Then let's go."

We exit the storage closet, heading for the stairs.

"I thought I was dead," he says. "Hell, I thought you were dead, too."

"They can't get rid of me that easy."

"I know. Trust me."

We reach the first floor, passing through the lobby and stepping out the shattered entrance. We move less than three strides before a large electronic billboard mounted to the side of a building in front of us flickers to life.

My stomach churns.

I'm going to puke.

The footage shows the inside of the warehouse Blaine and I were in only hours ago. Replacing the headless spy strapped to the metal chair, is Chloe. The skin around one of her eyes is shaded purple, and blood spills steadily out of each nostril.

Damn it!

Damn it, damn it, damn it!

My knees smack against the sidewalk. I can't breathe. I'm going to suffocate.

Something like this was bound to happen. I never should have left. I'm stupid.

Stupid, stupid, stupid!

My chest threatens to cave in.

Behind Chloe, the psychopath who started this all stands with his sword placed up against her pale neck, "I know you're seeing this, Jason." He grins, his tone victorious. "Did you really think this party could end without us seeing each other? I am the guest of honor, after all."

Chloe struggles, her gnashed teeth stained with blood.

Mills steps out in front of her, slowly approaching the camera. His sword drags behind him, "Come to warehouse A, or she dies. Bring anyone with you, and she dies. I have eyes everywhere, so don't think I won't notice. God vs. Lucifer. It's going to be magnificent. Once you're gone, I will finally be able to start this world anew."

"Jason!" Chloe screams out of view. "Don't do it! Take Blaine and go!"

Absolute refusal. I made a promise that I'd never let anything bad happen to her again.

I can't leave.

I won't.

Mills laughs. It embodies glee and anticipation. "You have one hour." He steps behind her. "If you aren't here, I'll cut her pretty little head off. Don't worry, though." He smooths his fingers across her chest. "I'll have my fun first."

The stream ends.

I see nothing but red, threatening my sanity.

Blaine turns, his face mirroring my own. "Let's go kill that evil bastard."

"No." My fists tremble. "You heard what he said. I have to show up alone."

"But he'll kill you."

"I knew what saving you would risk."

"Don't be stupid. He's an old, withering freak whose head isn't on straight. We can trick him."

"Yeah, maybe him, but not all the soldiers he has watching us right now."

"I wouldn't be able to forgive myself if you died for saving me."

"Stop arguing. We're running out of time. You can help in other ways."

"Like how?"

"I need you to reactivate the AA guns. After that, try to find anyone you can and head to the warehouse to clean up what's left."

He still wants to fight me on this, but he bites his tongue. "Is this goodbye?"

I don't say anything, moving in and giving him a hug instead. "After Simon died, I didn't think I'd have another best friend. Guess I was wrong, wasn't I?"

He lets out a sigh, "That sounds so final."

"The quicker you are, the better my chances. Just hurry.

"I will. Look, when I was in there, I found an old friend of ours."

"Who?"

He slips two things into my pocket. "It won't make you immortal, but it's the next best thing. I was going to use it on myself if I, well. . . you know."

There's a bit of a chance now. "Thank you."

I let go and he sniffles. Without another word, we go separate ways.

CHAPTER THIRTY-TWO

I walk down a street cluttered in carnage. Both rage and fear work through me as I near the warehouse at the edge of town. There are too many possibilities, too many ways this could end.

Bodies take up most of the area. It makes the topic of death prevalent in my mind. My fear of demise plagues me, but my blinding lust to kill simmers the sting.

I imagine my dad by my side. He puts an arm around me.

"Give me strength," I mutter.

He rubs my shoulder. "I already have."

He asks about my life, and what has led up to this. He congratulates me on Chloe's pregnancy, and I halfheartedly chuckle, telling him that's not what he'd really say if he were here.

The warehouse comes into view as I turn down the end of the street.

The memory of my dad disappears.

I walk a couple hundred more yards before stopping at the large doors. I glance back one last time, telling myself that everything will be okay.

The chances of killing him and making it out alive are slim.

I clear my throat, taking hold of a metal handle and sliding the entrance open.

The inside is illuminated by the florescent lights above. On each side of the warehouse, two Reapers stand guard, shotguns in hand. Chloe and Mills are waiting in the center.

Four cameras are set up at each corner.

"Men are so easy." Mills smiles. One of his Reapers steps behind me and slides the entrance shut again. "All you have to do is steal their piece of meat and they'll come running."

"You're pathetic," I say.

He tilts his head to the side, flashing a grin. "You could've escaped Boston. I never would've found you, yet you came here because your tiny, primal brain needs a mate, and you say I'm pathetic?"

Between the cameras, the Reapers, and the immenent threat of death, my venomous hate flows free, "The entire time I've had the displeasure of knowing you, I've concluded you're just an egotistical old fool with a warped God complex. You crave attention because it keeps you going."

"That's the most ridiculous thing I've ever heard leave your mouth."

"Do you ever listen to yourself? I mean, honestly. Do you hear the insanity that pours between your disgusting lips? You're sick. Sick in the head. These past two years have fried your brain. You hear me, old man?"

He laughs. His smile looks like it might split his face open. "If that were true, the Maiden's Touch would have killed me, just like it's going to kill you."

"You've had so many opportunities to end me, but you didn't. You could've bombed Boston months ago, but you didn't. You could've killed me while I was trapped in the Estate, but you didn't." My breath turns heavy. "You could've had your men kill me on the way here, but you didn't! Do you know why, Joseph? It's because you crave this, you psychotic bastard! I'm going to rip your head off! Do you hear me? I'm really gonna prove you're mortal!"

His expression is replaced with malice. He grabs the chair Chloe's tied to and drags it to the side of the warehouse. "I want any weapons he has confiscated. Make sure he's free of EMPs."

Pitiful. The four Reapers approach me and I grimace. "So this isn't a fight? All I see right now is the twisted start of cat and mouse."

"I am superior to you, so yes."

A smile spreads across my face. The soldiers grope me. "We'll see about that."

They take my gun, my knife, and my radio.

"Is that all?" Mills inquires.

"He has a little rock in his pocket," one notes.

I burst, "Don't touch it!"

"Give it to me," Mills orders.

The solider rips the object away, tossing it to his leader. He catches it, and after scrutinizing, laughs some more. "Is it sentimental?"

Idiots.

I notice Chloe subtly loosening her restraints.

Mills nears the center of the room, an aura of infamy emitting from his frame. "I want the cameras back on. The surviving souls of this nation must witness the death of the Devil and his whore."

The Reapers approach the equipment, toying around with some buttons.

Chloe's gaze meets mine. There's unease. She's worried about me, about herself, and our little us, but she doesn't need to be.

Not with what I have up my sleeve.

One Reaper clears his throat. "Broadcast starting in five, four, three, two, one."

Everything that's happened these past two years has led to this. Inside an empty warehouse at the edge of town. Maybe it should have been more exotic, or gritty, but I know one thing for sure.

I'm going to drown this room in his blood.

He's going to pay.

Revenge isn't overrated or overdone.

It's a necessity.

Mills stares at me. His brown eyes narrow to slits. "Let us begin."

CHAPTER THIRTY-THREE

The tension in the room splits as he charges. His blade screeches across the floor.

I smile, dodging his strike. I counter with a punch to the face.

He stammers back, swinging again. But only one of us has had combat training.

I duck, using all my might to tackle him to the floor. He punches me twice before using the handle of his weapon to bash my nose.

Blood starts to spill from me. I pin him down, hammering my palm into his throat.

Something crushes inside his esophagus. He sputters a moment before recovering entirely.

I hit harder and faster

A hand pulls me from behind.

I'm pried from the psychopath and forced to the floor.

A Reaper's foot crashes into my face. A flurry of kicks ensue.

My world flashes white.

The Reaper kicks at my ribs and cracks a few. All air escapes my lungs and I gasp.

I grab his leg on the last strike and take him to the ground, climbing on top and ripping the gas mask from his face. I dig my thumbs deep into his eye sockets, feeling the inside of his head.

"Jason!" Chloe blurts.

Mills' sword breaches my flesh, blasting through my abdomen like paper. I let out a sharp groan, my eyes moving down to the steel tip protruding through my back and out my stomach.

The Reaper beneath me screams as my thumbs retract from his sockets.

Blood dribbles from my mouth.

Chloe sobs.

Mills rips the blade out, kicking the small of my back.

I smack against the floor. Scarlet pools around my body.

Mills approaches the thrashing Reaper. With one swift movement, he decapitates him. "What a spoil."

My stare finds Chloe. Her emerald green eyes flood with tears. She's not even trying to hide the fact that she's almost out of her restraints.

"It's. . . okay," I mutter. Blood spits out between my lips.

Mills stands over me. Success gleams in his eyes. "Two years. For two years you've been a thorn in my side. Who knew it would be so satisfying? Easy?"

I carefully bend my leg so that my foot touches my hip. "You —sick—fu—"

"Shh, no profanity. There are children watching at home."

I lower my hand to my shoe. The agony is so severe I puke blood.

He stares into one of the cameras. "Do you see where this has led you all? Down a path of misery and death, and for what? It would have been an honor to breed for me, and while some of you will still get that opportunity, most of you will die beneath my heel."

I slide part of my shoe off, reaching inside.

"I am God, and I will reclaim my world," he continues to the audience.

I pull out a pill and a syringe.

This is for everyone you've killed.

The Reapers yell out, but they are not fast enough. I plunge the needle into my body and release the serum inside. Then, I pop the pill in my mouth.

As if it were just an illusion, the pain in my stomach fades.

My flesh knits back together.

Mills' eyes widen. *"I said confiscate everything!"*

Chloe breaks free, lunging at the nearest Reaper. She wrestles the shotgun out of his hands.

I roll out of the way as Mills swings his blade once again.

A blast erupts. I jump to my feet. A Reaper collapses without a face.

More gunfire explodes from the other side of the room. I take a shotgun blast to the arm. It shreds, but the flesh immediately regenerates, and I grab Mills just in time for the next shot, turning his body to take the brunt end of it.

Chloe turns and pumps my attacker full of pellets.

Mills throws the back of his head against my nose, freeing my grip. He turns, and with another swing of his sword, severs my arm.

The limb drops to the ground.

I step back, the pain leaving as fresh bone forms at the remnant.

Blood leaks from my eyes.

Laughter. Hysterical laughter. The familiar mania takes over.

Mills swings again.

I dodge. My knuckles smash against his teeth and I throw my forehead against his face.

Black blood sputters from his face.

Chloe fires at the last Reaper. The blast hits him in the shoulder.

He drops his gun and charges, too close for her fire again. He rips the gun from her hands and throws it across the room.

She pries the mask from his face.

He chokes her.

Mills digs his blade into my thigh.

I bite into his neck, tearing away at the flesh.

Chloe gets thrown to the floor.

The Reaper rushes me.

I take the fresh, blade-like bone jutting from the base of my arm and use it as a weapon, thrusting it through the soldier's face and lifting him up off the ground.

Mills steps back, swinging his blade.

I use the Reaper as a shield. He's cut in half, and I fling his upper body to the ground.

"*Just die!*" Mills howls. He wildly attacks.

Chloe jumps on his back and claws at his eyes as I evade him.

He howls. I pry the sword from his hand. "Chloe!"

She jumps off him as I swing, but he ducks, tackling me to the floor.

My head smacks against the last Reaper's detached lower body. Out of my peripheral vision, I see a hand grenade attached to his waist.

Mills punches down on my face.

I reach for the explosive.

He screams, "*Die! Die! Die! Die!*"

My vision tinges different colors. I pry the grenade from the body and unpin it, bashing it through Mills' teeth and into his mouth.

His eyes widen.

I hurl him off me.

The force of the explosion pushes me forward. His head explodes, black gore flying across the room. Chloe is forced to the ground.

My eyes dart over. "Are you okay?"

"Yeah, I think so."

I get to my feet. My arm is completely healed.

I move my fingers in awe, psychotic giggles escaping my mouth.

Mills lies in a puddle of blood. His head all the way down to his ribcage is nonexistent.

That's when I see it.

An EMP grenade stitched to an exposed lung.

What the hell?

Black gel-like liquid waterfalls from his wounds. I rush in, grabbing at the device.

He throws his hands up, catching me in the jaw.

My teeth dig into my tongue, but the pain fades as I plunge my hands into his exposed frame. I pull at the device, but the serum in his body refuses to let go. Black tar smothers the grenade as I pull.

He slams a fist into my jaw, breaking some fingers.

I pull harder.

He grabs a hold of my throat.

I grit my teeth.

He squeezes.

I pull.

His body is about to close when the device finally gives way. A chunk of his lung comes with it.

I try to toss the grenade to Chloe, but he kicks it out of my hand, a new face already forming. The EMP flies across the room and smacks against one of the walls.

His eyes take shape. The three of us rush forward. He grabs me by the hood and pulls me back, sprinting to Chloe as she dives for the grenade. He contacts her mid-air and the two of them tumble to the floor.

I kick him in his fresh face as he reaches.

He jerks out a concealed dagger and thrusts it into my leg.

The pain is short lived.

Chloe reaches for the device, but he yanks his weapon out of me and stabs it into her arm. He pulls it out and aims for her stomach, but I kick his wrist.

It snaps.

He drops the blade.

"Do it!" I yell, dropping down and pinning him. "Do it, now!"

She activates it.

Mills screams.

The blast goes off.

I collapse off him. My body thrashes. The Rebirth within me reacts to the pulse.

My stomach is about to rupture. I'm scared my heart will explode.

Chloe drops at my side. "It's okay, you're okay."

I puke blood. It's thick and spatters against the ground.

She reels a bit.

The pain suddenly stops.

Mills is curled up next to us, sucking in as much air as possible.

"That fail safe was foolish," he says to himself. "Stupid, stupid, *stupid.*"

Wiping red from the corners of my lips, I mutter. "Will you shut the hell up for once in your life?"

He rolls over, his suit torn to pieces, "You have no idea what you've just done. . ."

I stagger to my feet. My head spins. "No, I'm very well aware."

He whimpers as I grab him by the hair, dragging him to a camera.

"This is your God?" I ask, unamused. "Pathetic. All I see is a man."

As I hold him in my grip, I can't help but reflect on all the suffering he caused. Without the Maiden's Touch, he's nothing. So why did we all fear him all our lives? This is the man who we couldn't speak ill of without execution. The man who has statues of himself all throughout the country where we were expected to worship him. The man who ordered the hit on my parents.

A power-hungry mortal. All along, it's been him; a sad old man.

"Please," he begs. "Please, I'll give you all amnesty. You and your people can live with liberty far away from here. We will never cross paths again."

"Amnesty?" I fight my laughter. "You want to give me and my people absolution?" I stare into the camera with wide eyes. "Do you believe this man? After everyone he's ravaged, killed, and tortured, he wants to pardon *us* and let *us* walk away?"

"We can divide the nation in half," he pleads. "We won't bother each other. You have my word."

Chloe stands behind me, handing me his sword.

I let go of him. He drops to his knees.

"Say hi to Matthew for me," I mock.

Millions of people watch me swing the blade into his neck. I rip it out and plant it back in, a rageful howl beaming from my lips. His headless corpse collapses at my feet.

Chloe disables each of the cameras.

I toss the sword to the floor, grabbing my rock out of Mills' pocket and putting it in my own.

"Did we actually win. . .?" Chloe asks.

I glance around the room. There's nothing but corpses. "I think so."

"How did you get Rebirth? I haven't seen a drop of it since before the Estate."

"Blaine found it in the hospital. I don't think our medical staff knew what it was, so they left it alone."

She smiles, stumbling over and embracing me. "Good."

Blood oozes from her stab wound. I take a deep breath. "Let's go get you patched up."

She nods.

Over. It's finally over. This isn't a dream.

We won.

The two of us walk to the large doors. I'm about to slide one open, but through the small gap in the middle, something moves.

I carefully put my eye up to it. "No... No, please no."

"What's wrong?"

Hundreds of armed Saints surround the warehouse.

"Military," I mutter, backing away from the door.

"*Heretic!*" someone yells through a megaphone. "*Step out now!*"

I panic. My rampant thoughts crash inside my skull.

"What are we going to do?" Chloe goes paler than she already is.

I hurry over to the dead Reaper who confiscated my radio. I bring it to my mouth. "Blaine, you there?"

Moments go by before he replies. "Just about to activate the AA guns. You're okay?"

My heart sinks. "You aren't close?"

"No, security here was tight. Did you save her?"

I don't reply.

"Jason?"

"I'm here..."

"What's going on?"

"Hold up..."

I clip the radio to my belt, taking in the room. There's only one entrance and a small window near the back that only Chloe could fit through.

A lump forms in my throat.

The realization hits me all at once.

Death has finally caught up to me.

"Jason." Chloe snaps me out of it. "We need to hurry."

I hold back my tears, grabbing her hand and leading her to the window. It's just above my head, so I have to get on my tip toes to see if the coast is clear.

It is.

"What are you doing?" she asks.

"You're going through the window."

"But that's only big enough—" She stops. "No way. There's no way you're serious."

"Please don't argue."

Her face turns bright red. "Shut up. I'm not leaving you here."

I place my hand on her stomach. Blood spills from my eyes. "Please?"

Her shoulders shake, "Don't make me do this."

"You have to."

"No, there has to be another way."

Gazing around a second time, I pray a magical new exit appears.

There isn't.

More tears.

"Please," I beg. "You have to get far away from here."

"They're going to kill you."

"I know that."

"I wish we would've just left."

I heave out a sigh, my nose runny. "We would've just lived in fear."

"I'd rather live in fear than lose you."

I embrace her, "I promise everything is going to be okay."

"I can't do this."

"Yes, you can."

The solider with the megaphone blurts, *"Forty seconds!"*

I part from her, getting back up on my tip toes and sliding the window open.

She protests some more, but I hush her, "Please."

Her knees shake, but that doesn't stop her from cradling my face. For a moment, we stare at each other. Then I kiss her one last time before lifting her up.

"I love you. . ." I say, almost in a whisper.

This isn't real.

She pulls herself up and with another desperate look, says, "Please don't make me do this."

My eyes tell her everything. She needs to live for more than just me.

I smile. "Just say it back, dummy."

"I love you too. Always."

Chloe puts a leg out the window, and slowly turns her head. Our eyes meet one last time. Then she jumps and disappears out of sight.

I'll never see her again.

"*Twenty seconds!*"

I face the door.

"Jay," Blaine's voice pours through my radio. "Talk to me. You're giving me a panic attack."

I shudder out a sigh, blood dripping from my face. I unclip the radio, "Keep them safe."

"What the hell is that supposed to mean?"

I turn it off and toss it to the floor.

My legs threaten to give out.

I walk to the entrance as the Saint outside counts down from ten.

She's getting far away from here.

Don't worry.

It's okay.

My hand trembles as I pull the rock she gave me out of my pocket.

I then reach for the handle.

I'm scared.

"*Four! Three! Two!*"

I slide it open, the spotlight from a helicopter shines down on me.

Hundreds of soldiers stand at the ready. Their weapons are pointed at me.

I take a few steps out.

The sun is starting to rise.

The Saint with the megaphone raises his arm in the air. He says something, but I don't hear him. Instead, I rub my thumb across the rock.

It's okay.

I remember the night at the harbor when Chloe pulled me into the cold water, kissing me with her loving embrace. At that moment, everything was perfect.

I smile.

All I can hope for, is that one day, I'll see her pretty, green eyes again.

"Open fire!"

First my stomach, then my face.

Bullets tear me apart.

EPILOGUE
TEN YEARS LATER

The gray sky sets a somber mood. The autumn leaves blow around in the brisk November air.

People roam the streets freely, not a care in the world. Some just got done shopping, others are getting off work. In the distance, a group of younger kids are ordering from an ice cream truck.

The Sweet Tooth.

Valentine's favorite.

"Well." Chloe wipes her eyes. "I guess now is as good a time as any."

She opens her car door and steps out into the cool breeze.

"Uncle Blaine," Val calls from the backseat. "Can we get ice cream after this?"

I gaze at him through the rearview mirror. He looks just like him: dirty blond hair and a sharp face. He has Chloe's green eyes but has a mix of both their attitudes.

"Are you going to hold your mom's hand?"

"Mhmm."

"Yeah, then I can get you some ice cream, little dude"

Chloe opens his door, and he steps out.

I follow them. The shades that cover my eyes block out the wind.

We pass through the black gates. Dark crosses stand vigilant over those they mark...

Chloe and Val take the lead. I slowly trail them as they head toward the back of the cemetery.

I was too late to save him... I sped to the warehouse as fast as I could. The Saints were retreating since their helicopters were shot down all throughout the city, but that didn't matter, not when Jason was lying dead in the grass, his body broken.

I held him in my arms.

Despite there not being much left, a smile was still on his face.

I have to prepare myself for this every year. No matter how much I tell myself I'm not going to cry, it always happens.

Emotions are dumb.

I take a deep breath, watching the warm mist leave my mouth. I approach Val and Chloe. They stand in front of a black cross. A stone slab beneath it has his name on it.

Jason Pinder.

He didn't get a big memorial, or any statues. He wouldn't have been into any of that crap. He didn't do it for the fame or the recognition. He did it for her.

He was always destined for this.

Val lets go of his mother's hand, kneeling and wiping the dead leaves off the slab with his small hand. He doesn't say anything for a bit, but eventually he croaks, "Hey, dad."

Tears.

Two minutes.

A new record.

Val tells him how much he loves him. He wishes he could've hugged his dad at least once. It's a bit much for me, but I stay strong, giving him a little hug once he's finished.

Chloe likes alone time when she has her words with Jay, so I go next.

"Hey, man. . . I know I don't always have a lot to say, but I miss you and your stupid face." My voice is weak. "I've kept them safe, just like you asked."

I eventually say my goodbyes, taking Val and stepping away.

Chloe does her thing, and we watch from a distance.

He would always tell me how scared he was to die. That it would be lonely. I'd like to believe that I found him smiling because he got over it and found peace before the end.

Val looks up. "Do you think dad liked ice cream?"

I shrug. "I don't know, but you know what I do know?"

"Hmm?"

"That he'd be proud of you."

"Cringe."

"Hey, what did I tell you? Emotion is *cringe* every day *but* today."

He chuckles, wiping away the tears in his eyes. "I know."

I know he'd be happy with what we've built. Now, you can say whatever you want without the fear of getting a bullet lodged in your skull. You can practice any ideology, religion, and there isn't a curfew.

I haven't seen a checkpoint since the night we took Seattle.

Not everything is figured out, but that's okay because we're getting there, and that's all that matters.

An hour goes by. Chloe joins us. Her mascara is smeared.

Val gives her a hug, and the three of us leave the cemetery.

Until next year, Jay. . .

A sense of peace surges through my veins as I guide them to the ice cream truck. For a moment, I allow myself to forget all the hell I've been through, all the scars and damage done to my mind and body.

I allow myself to live, and that's all thanks to him.

Jason Pinder.

The man who changed the world.

ACKNOWLEDGMENTS

Man, three years later and here we are. . . It's crazy to think I started writing this trilogy when I was just fourteen. First and foremost, I'd like to apologize for such a long wait — since publishing Mutiny back in 2019, my life has been filled with ups and down, mostly regarding my mental health and then some external situations that weren't very fun to deal with. On the bright side, Amnesty was a great outlet for expressing my fears, anger, and desires. A lot of Jason's dread and anguish through the finale was very real to me, and I'm grateful that you stuck around to the end and finished his journey.

I'd like to start this off by thanking my editor, Stacey Smekofske. In High School, I'd never shut up about having written a book at such a young age. Stacey had two daughters who attended one of my classes, and after one of the many instances of me bragging up a storm, they proudly told me that their mom was a professional editor and would TOTALLY love to work with me (since at the time, I had only finished my first draft and nothing else). I eagerly reached out, and after reading a snippet from Revolt, she agreed to take on the project. Stacey, you have been so much more than just an editor. You've taught me about the publishing world, how to get into the best stores, how to boost sales, you've done it all. Most importantly though, you've always been there when I needed advice and motivation to keep working. Thank you.

Next, I'd like to thank my wonderful parents who have supported me through thick and thin — especially through all the recent unexpected hurdles. Mom, you're a saint, and despite hating violence with a burning passion, you've beta read both Revolt and Mutiny. I spared her from this one. . . for obvious reasons. . . but I'm so grateful for you and all the cheerleading you've done. Dad you, on the other hand, have been one of my best critics. You've always told me when things were too unrealistic, or flat out dumb; even though the feedback was unappreciated in the moment, your advice and wisdom has better shaped my series (especially with Amnesty, which I'm most proud of). I love you both.

I'd also like to thank my beautiful fiancée, Natalie, for all the amazing feedback and support she's given me over the years. From helping me craft my female characters to giving me advice on how to create the ending, you have done so much for this final book. I love you to the moon and back, and I couldn't ask for a better partner.

To my siblings. Lexi, I want to thank you for drawing me some of the coolest fan-art ever. Aubrie, you're one of the biggest hype-up gals I know — it's almost impossible not to be motivated once this girl has cheered you on. Nathan, you've done absolutely nothing for this series, and you tend to steal my work chair to game on your PC, BUT. . . you've always been an amazing person to sit down with and decompress with after a long day — from the many all-nighters we've pulled binging anime to simply just gaming together, you've saved me from a lot of built up stress. Seth, you've helped more on the mental side of things, which in the long run actually helped me be able to finish this trilogy. Finally, August, when I worked for you, you allowed me so many days off to make a deadline, which helped out more than you could possibly imagine.

Last but not least, I'd like to thank you, the reader, for all the support you've shown. Just buying and reading this book means the world to me. That isn't to sound cliché at all because I know every author says it, but I really mean it. Nothing can top the feeling I get when I see one of my novels has a new review, or when someone asks me when my next book will be launched since they're dying to read it. I love you all. Seriously.

Now, I bet some of you are wondering what's next for me now that The Revolt Trilogy is finished. Well, I'm pleased to announce that I have a new novel in the works at this very moment. It's titled When God Grins, and it's a switch in genre, but I'm confident that it'll be an adrenaline pumping fever dream that will leave you with a dropped jaw. I'm hoping to launch it early next year if all goes according to plan. I'll reveal more details and set a release date.

Until next time! Stay safe, stay healthy, and don't forget to take care of yourself. You deserve it.

Benjamin Vogt

ABOUT THE AUTHOR

Benjamin Vogt was just sixteen when he published his first novel, Revolt. Years later, the now twenty-year-old has a finished trilogy under his belt, and he is working on his next novel. In his free time, Ben loves to play video games, watch an unhealthy amount of anime, and spend time with his friends, family, and fiancée.

COMING SOON

WHEN GOD GRINS

A DARK FANTASY
BY BENJAMIN VOGT

....

2023

www.ingramcontent.com/pod-product-compliance
Ingram Content Group UK Ltd.
Pitfield, Milton Keynes, MK11 3LW, UK
UKHW042003230426
12048UKWH00009B/521